Mazie

Shayna Astor

Edited by NiceGirlNaughtyEdits
Edited by Beth Hudson
Cover Designer Fine's Fine Designs
Formatting Fine's Fine Designs

Mazie

From the Author

Mazie is a full-length, novel that features strong language, mature situations, explicit sexual scenes, alcohol use, mentions of death, grieving, a college campus hostage situation, a shooting, and mental health. This book is intended for readers age 18 and up. While Mazie can be read as a stand alone, it is recommended to read the series in order.

Thank you so much for reading my novel! I hope you enjoy reading it, as much as I enjoyed writing it!

Other Books by Shayna Astor

Hot & Cold

Shattered Pieces

Own Me (A dark romance)

Off Limits (Book 1 in the Limits Series)

Love Me Not

Faking Perfection: A Brighton High School Reunion

Olivia (Book 1 in The Baker Sibling Series)

Dedication

For anyone who had a friend but always knew there was
more to it than just platonic feelings.

Chapter 1
Mazie

How did this happen? How did they surpass me in life?

As I dance and sing at the top of my lungs with my baby sisters at Alina's wedding, those questions keep circling in the back of my mind. I can't believe they're both married now. And Liv has a baby. It doesn't even feel real.

It's not that I'm jealous. Well, not entirely. How could I not be when I so desperately want to be a wife and mother? But I'm not angry jealous. I love them both dearly, and I'm incredibly happy for them finding their perfect matches, finding their forevers.

But I'd be lying if I said I wasn't a little sad for me.

The free-flowing alcohol helps numb the sting a little bit. As does this carefree moment with our arms around each other as we scream-sing a song from when we were younger.

There is a sadness weighing me down, but it has nothing to do with my sisters passing me in life's accomplishments and everything to do with who's missing.

Our parents.

They would have been over the moon at each wedding and the most doting grandparents the world has ever seen for Liv's baby. I can hear Mom now, calling Jordanna her baby's baby.

It's not often that I think about how unfair life has been to me and my siblings by tearing them away from us, and so brutally. But the thought has been on my mind more lately.

Especially for Liv. She had the least time with them, the least time to get Mom's sage advice and Dad's handy skills. The least fatherly protection and motherly love.

It's where my brother, Eli, and I have stepped in the best we could. It wasn't even a conscious decision; we knew what had to be done and got to it. I know I overstep my bounds sometimes, but I'm a worrier at heart.

Their murder made it hard for me to trust people. It's why I gave Jameson such a hard time at first. He's an outsider, and I don't like opening our family to outsiders. In fact, I don't really like outsiders at all. Which is a large reason I tend to do most of my work for the café from home.

It's also probably why Zach is my best friend. We've known each other since we were kids. He's not just a good person, but he's a safe place for me too.

And that's probably how I pick his voice out above the music. He's urgently trying to express something, but what, I can't tell. Concern takes over the fun, and I hope he's okay. I saw him earlier, downing drink after drink. Not something he does often, since he rarely takes a day off from work.

As the song ends and changes to something a little slower, I make my way toward the tables and find him seated with Eli and Cameron, the two of them shoulder to shoulder in front of him.

I walk over and push them apart as a waiter brings over a cup of steaming coffee.

Kneeling in front of Zach, I put my hands on his to get him to look at me. But instead, he sways slightly, a stupid smirk on his face. He's three sheets to the wind.

"Mazie! There she is." The words come out way too loud and a bit slurred. His eyes are red and glossy.

"Hey, Zach. What's going on?" I try to make my voice sound as calming as possible, even when I'm borderline panicked. I don't know what to do with a drunken Zach. While I've seen it several times over the course of our friendship, it's been years, and he's far bulkier than he ever was back in high school and college.

"I had a few drinks. They were so good. And I have to tell you that I—"

"He wanted to tell you that he was having a great time and that you look beautiful," Eli interjects while clapping a hand on Zach's shoulder at the same time that Cameron shoves the coffee into Zach's hands.

My eyes narrow, and I know they're hiding something, but I don't push, not wanting to start anything at my sister's wedding.

Standing, I turn around and lean into Eli. "You're going to have to help me get him home. You know that, right?"

"Yup. Already figuring out if we should let him hang here or try to get him out sooner as opposed to later."

I glance over my shoulder to take another look at Zach's condition. "Let's see how the coffee treats him. But he needs a babysitter."

"You or me?"

"If you don't mind, I'm going to ask you, because if he falls, I can't catch him."

"I'm not sure I can either. He's a big dude." While Eli has some muscles himself, Zach is broad, with muscles on muscles. While it's not usually my thing, I've always felt like it suits Zach.

And I can't deny how safe I feel with him, and not just because he's a cop. He could pummel anybody who tried to hurt me. There's certainly been a time or two he's wanted to when some guy I was dating broke my heart. Most can't handle the dead parents and how that has come to affect me on a daily basis. Such as the crippling anxiety I just can't rid myself of.

But Zach was there through it all. He lets me be me. That's why he's such an amazing friend, and I'm so lucky to have him.

Turning back to check on Zach again, I find him passed out on the table, mouth open and surely snoring. I've always promised not to tell any future girlfriends that the man snores like a Mack truck roaring down the highway.

"I think he'll be okay for a while, if you don't mind sitting with him. Just in case he wakes up." I bite my lip and raise my eyebrows toward Eli. I already know he'll agree. He's a good man and a better brother. But I still feel guilty asking since it's his sister's wedding too.

"Not a problem. You know I'm not much for dancing anyway. Plus, you girls looked like you were having fun."

I notice that Liv and Alina are still on the dance floor, and a smile pulls up the corners of my lips. "Yeah. We were."

Things have been tense, off and on, over the past...well...several years, really. But especially when Jameson came into Liv's life. And again, when Cam was first back. That motherly role hasn't gone away just because they're adults. They still don't have Mom around and I feel like I need to be there in whatever way I can be.

It's nice for us to have this time together when the stressors of life and things that have been said or done are far behind us.

Because the first time one of the bonehead brothers-in-law messes up, I'll be the first to jump to my sister's defense.

Chapter 2
Zach

The pounding in my head is what wakes me. It's like a jackhammer has taken root in my brain.

How much did I drink last night?

Sitting up in bed, the sheets pool around my waist, and the heel of my hand finds my temple. I can barely open my eyes against the bright light pouring in through the blinds.

How did I get home?

I finally open my eyes enough to take in my surroundings. And the first thing I notice is that I'm not actually at home. The pink sheets on the bed are not my black ones. Nor is the frilly comforter.

But I know whose it is without having to crawl out of bed.

I've seen this room a hundred times, slept in it a handful.

"The fuck did I do last night?" I mumble to myself.

It's then I notice I have no shirt on. Lifting the sheet, I find I'm not wearing pants either. Just my boxer briefs.

There's no way Mazie changed me and got me into bed on her own. I have at least fifty pounds of muscle on her. She wouldn't even be able to support me drunk.

Which means, at the very *least*, Eli had to have helped.

Great. Now I owe the family for getting wasted at the most recent wedding.

It just became too much, and the alcohol seemed to help. Another baby Baker has gotten married, leaving only one sister. Mazie's the oldest. She should have gone first. And...it could have been us.

But she doesn't even notice me.

The number of times she's friend-zoned me is more than I can count, and it hurts more and more each time.

The simple fact is that I'm pretty sure I've been in love with her since we were fourteen.

She was never gross or icky to me, always my closest friend and confidante. And somehow at that young age, I realized what I felt for her went beyond just friendship, beyond what I felt for her sisters, even the other people I was friends with, including other girls. She's always been special and had a place in my heart that was solely hers.

With another groan, I rip off the sheet. I'm just about to throw my legs over the side of the bed when the door opens.

Mazie walks in, her auburn hair in perfect ringlets. Her sapphire eyes widen and sparkle as she looks at me. "Oh! I didn't know you were awake yet."

Though I'm sure she tries not to, I watch her gaze track over my body, landing on my boxers. Quickly, I pull the sheet back over myself as one corner of my mouth tips up.

"Just woke up. How bad was I last night?" I look at her through my fingers as I cover my face in shame.

"Not the worst I've seen you, but pretty plastered. How's your head?"

"Terrible."

"Here." She steps forward and extends a coffee mug and a glass of water, and then turns her palm up, two aspirin sitting in the center.

I take the coffee and set it on the nightstand, grabbing the pills and tossing them in my mouth before taking a swig of water to wash them down. Then I realize how parched I am and chug the glass. With a quick wipe of my mouth with the back of my hand, I trade the glass for the mug.

After I give it a slight blow, I take the first sip. "Mmm. Thank you." The coffee at Mazie's is always delicious. I'm sure she and the girls all bring it home from the shop. Why wouldn't they? It's the best coffee in town and it's far better than anything you can buy at the grocery store.

"You're welcome." She sits on the edge of the bed and looks down at her lap. Something's bothering her, but I can't tell what.

"Just get it out." I take another big sip of the amazingly dark liquid. While my stomach wants to gnaw at itself, the warmth and caffeine are already helping my hangover.

"There just seemed to be something you wanted to tell me, and the guys wouldn't let you. Or I guess, just kind of interrupted before you got a chance to say anything." Her sapphire gaze rolls up to meet mine.

But the problem with how much I drank is I don't remember much beyond a certain point in the night. And nothing stands out as something I needed to tell Mazie.

"I wish I could tell you what it was, but I honestly don't remember. There's nothing there now, so I can't imagine what it was last night."

Her shoulders slump, and she looks disappointed. But then it's gone as she straightens, flips some curls behind her shoulders, and clasps her hands in her lap. Put together Mazie is here and she's likely to stay.

"That's okay. I was just curious. It seemed important, and I wanted to make sure we talked about whatever it was. Once you're ready, come on out, and I'll make some breakfast."

"You don't have to do that. Or at least let me cook since you let me stay." I make some mean scrambled eggs. But that's kind of the extent of my breakfast making capabilities.

"Nonsense. I'll make some pancakes to soak up whatever's still in your system." She pats my leg and stands. I know she tries to hide it, but her gaze rakes over my chest again. I can't help but smile.

"You're too good to me, M." She always has been.

"I'll go get started." Without another word, she's out the door, closing it quietly behind her.

One more sip of coffee, and a wide stretch, and I'm able to get out of bed. It's then I notice a pile of clothes on the dresser. The corner of my mouth tips down as I take in the clothes. A pair of drawstring pants and one of my old shirts. I must have left it here at some point. Probably last summer when I helped her paint the living room and it was hot as balls.

The pants are surely Eli's. It's not that he lives far, but I know Mazie keeps some of his clothes handy in case he needs to spend the night. Which I'm sure he spent it somewhere after the wedding instead of going home.

I wonder if I took his spot. He won't mind, but I feel bad if I put him or anybody else in the family out.

Seeing as it was Cam and Alina's wedding, I'm sure he didn't stay with them, so the only other option is that he slept on Mazie's couch, which I doubt, or he went over to Mansion Penshir. Jameson has been welcomed into the fold pretty well by now so I'm sure it was no issue.

I'll have to check in with Eli later and thank him, make sure he knows I'm sorry for getting so fucked up. And probably apologize to Cam too.

Between him and Alina, I know she'll just shrug it off and tell me it's no big deal.

Hopefully, I didn't make too big of a fool of myself. I'll have to find out before I go talk to them. Or maybe I should wait until after they've been married for a few hours?

I'm sure there's some sort of protocol here, but I have no idea what it is and what's right.

With a sigh, I pull on the pants and shrug on the shirt. It's a bit tight in the arms.

I pad out into the living room and run a hand through my hair before settling at the table while Mazie putters in the kitchen. She'll refuse my help even if I offer it, and being vertical and on my feet doesn't lend to me wanting to help right now.

As though summoned by my thoughts, she comes over and refills my coffee cup, pushing it a little closer to me.

"Drink up."

"Sorry I was such a mess last night. And that you had to put up with me being here."

"Oh, stop. You're never a bother. I was a little worried about you, but Eli assured me you'd be fine." He, of all people, would know how far up to and beyond my limit I would go. That's what happens when you basically grow up drinking together.

Eli and Mazie are my closest friends. The Bakers are my second family. Enough so that their parents' brutal murder was what encouraged me to buckle down, stop dicking around in college, and focus my major. On criminal justice. Some may say it's cliche to join the police force after such a tragedy shook our tiny town, but it never sat right with me that it happened and how long it took to find the person responsible.

Plus, the protection I wanted to bestow on Mazie was something I couldn't do as an ordinary citizen. I know how much her life changed and her outlook on people has altered since then.

It's practically made her a recluse. I'm not sure she even has friends outside of me and her siblings. Not anymore. Her trust in people has diminished. Not that I can blame her. After what she went through, it's not hard to see why she lost the fun-loving party girl side of herself. At first, the change in her sliced deep, but now it's more of a nagging sting, a reminder of an old injury.

The smells coming from the kitchen make my mouth water. Alina may be the chef of the family, but their mom was always in the kitchen. They had home-cooked meals every night. Far different from my upbringing of fast food or microwave dinners. That was the most cooking Mom ever did, pressing the buttons on the microwave.

I try not to blame her. Life gave her a rough hand, raising me alone after Dad split. He, I do blame. A lot. He woke up one morning and just decided marriage and a kid weren't for him. Mom had to work two jobs to afford to stay in our house in Juniper Grove. She didn't want to tear me away from the friends I'd made, which were really just Mazie and Eli. But I always had a place in their home.

The home cooked meals I ate were Jenna Baker's. She was my second mom, and the only reason I never considered her first is because I knew how much my own mother was busting her ass for me. But Paul, he was the only father figure I ever had.

Their death hurt me almost as much as their own kids.

Without asking, I know the pancakes that M is whipping up are the same ones Jenna made every Saturday morning. I was lucky enough to be privy to their deliciousness from a young age, and even if I hadn't slept over the night before, I was welcomed into their home at seven in the morning.

"You look far away. What's going on?" Mazie slides a plate in front of me, her brow furrowed.

"Just reminiscing. That's all." I try not to bring up the past around any of the Bakers. It's easier than watching their demeanor change, their faces fall, their color drain.

Even over a decade later, it still happens.

Mazie has been doing better recently, finally able to say the word "family" again and reference her parents. They all had their own struggles, and I know they've all had therapy because of it.

I shovel a forkful of heavenly fluffy chocolate chip pancakes into my mouth. "Delicious, as always."

"Thank you." She flicks off the burner and sits opposite me at the table with her own plate and cup of coffee.

For a while, Mazie tried to make Alina and Liv pancakes on Saturdays like Jenna had. But not only was she not that great at it yet, it was too painful of a memory.

I wonder how she handles it now and if the process is dripping with dread and heartache.

"I promise to be out of your hair soon. I'll finish these up and go."

She rests her hand on mine and my heart races. "Stop. You're never a bother. You're my best friend, Zach. I like having you here."

I ignore the sting of only ever being her friend. "Except you surely weren't expecting me last night. And I wasn't exactly in prime condition. You shouldn't have to take care of me."

Her eyes twinkle as she looks at me. "I don't mind taking care of you."

Our gazes stay locked on one another's for a moment, and it feels like there's more between us.

But I clear my throat and shake the thought away.

Mazie could never be interested in me. She's made it clear that we are friends, and I'd hate to risk losing my closest friend by making an unwanted move.

It's why I keep my love for her to myself, close to the vest, and tell nobody. Not even Eli knows.

Chapter 3
Mazie

With Alina on her honeymoon, it requires me to be present in the café more than the few times a month I'm usually there.

When we bought the café, we all learned how to work the various coffee machines and the register. But only Alina knows how to bake well enough to sell everything. We've had to order out for the week she's away, and the quality is just sub-par.

Enough so that our regulars are asking when Alina will be back.

Not soon enough is the answer I say in my head. "Just a few days now," is the answer I give with a forced smile.

Thankfully, it's not prime tourist season, so we're not giving anybody except our regulars less than our best.

Liv's okay with me spending most of my time in the safety of my small office. It's really more of a closet that I've squeezed a small desk into. The girls use it for breaks sometimes, which is fine by me. They're welcome to my fortress any time they need it, but I know they both typically end up in the kitchen instead.

Though I've never explained my reclusiveness to Liv, she seems to understand my need to not be in the front of the house. She's always been very perceptive. It's something I don't give her enough credit for.

Ever since Liv's accident a few years ago, we've hired a few more staff members to help out in times of need. It's been great for the weekends that Jameson takes Liv and Jordanna down to the city.

But it makes writing schedules something I have to do more frequently and more in depth. Before, it was clear that Liv and Alina were in every day, and then they'd let me know what days they wanted an extra set of hands and who. Now, I try to make sure there are at least two other people on every single day.

It also makes our costs higher, but revenue is solid. Jameson begged me to let him look over the numbers to make sure we were on steady ground since it's Liv's livelihood, and even he was impressed with how well we've been able to make the little shop do.

That's what happens when you open the only decent café in a small town. We have people who come from Pineville City too, but that's because they want the small town, Mom-and-Pop feel.

While Juniper Grove is a small town, it's rich with local flare and even some history. There are amazing nature trails and it's a nice, quiet town just outside of a larger city. People like to frequent here for weekend getaways, and many who come, return in later years.

That's part of what makes me nervous about owning the shop. The tourists, the drifters, the strangers who come in and out. It's something I'm working on with my therapist and have been for years.

Most of the girls who work here are high school or college age, coming in to work their shifts after or before classes. They're all incredibly easy-going and sweet, which is good, because I'm not sure Liv would be able to handle a snotty attitude and would surely fire them on the spot.

As far as she's concerned, she's the only one who's allowed to have an attitude.

Once the schedules are set for the next two weeks, all classes and day-off requests accounted for, I take out the checkbook to start writing this week's paychecks.

I'm about to sign the second one when I hear a squeal out on the floor and jump up from my chair, pushing out into the dining area.

What I see warms my heart before the quick, icy tendril of jealousy wraps around my ribs.

Jameson brought Jordanna by and she toddles to Liv, who's squatting and has her arms outstretched, the proudest smile I've ever seen on her face.

Jordanna falls right into Liv's waiting arms, and she scoops up her daughter, giving her kisses all over her face until my niece giggles.

"I thought you'd want to see what we mastered today." Jameson closes the gap between them and puts an arm around Liv's waist, pulling her close and kissing the top of her head.

"I'm so proud of you, baby girl. What a big girl you're getting to be." She wipes a stray tear from her eye.

Though I try to keep the green monster at bay, it rears its ugly head in moments like this. Because I so desperately want what Liv has. The husband who loves me unconditionally and dotes on me constantly. The adorable baby who only has eyes for her mommy. At times, it makes things tense between me and Liv, which is entirely my problem and something I hate about myself.

I worry my time is running out. It's not that I'm old, per se. It's more that I feel my clock *tick, tick, ticking* and I have no suitors. With my detachment and inability to trust new people, it's going to take a while for somebody I'm dating to become a real love interest.

And I'll have to actually start dating again for that to happen.

Quickly, I shake the thought away and throw on my best smile. "Who's here to see her favorite auntie?" I reach into Liv's arms and pull Jordanna from her, tickling the sweet girl's little belly so she giggles again.

I swear this child has the best laugh.

"Favorite auntie, huh?" Liv crosses her arms and taps her toe on the ground. "You'll have to fight Alina for that title, you know."

"She's not here, so I get to say it. Yes, I do." I don't even look away from Jordanna as I talk in my baby voice.

"Did you see her new skill?"

"I did. She's growing up so fast."

"She really is." There's a waver to her voice. It must be hard to watch your first baby grow so quickly. And especially for her to do it without Mom and Dad around. I haven't spent enough time asking her how she's handling that.

Jameson leans down and whispers something in her ear, which makes her smile and nod. He's good to her, and good for her. I definitely didn't give him a fair chance at first.

But I'm hoping I've been able to make up for it in recent years.

Jordanna starts to wriggle in my arms, so I set her down. She takes careful steps right to Liv, wrapping her chubby little arms around my sister's legs.

Liv scoops her right up and smatters her face with kisses. Seeing my sister be a mom is truly amazing.

While she still insists on having pink streaks in her hair and wearing ripped jeans, she's so much more grown than I've given her credit for.

I find it somewhat ironic that, for years, I was the one who she turned to for advice, usually after Alina because they're just closer than Liv and

I ever have been, and at some point in the future, I'll be turning to Liv. Or at least, I hope so.

The family I so desperately want just feels farther and farther away these days.

The bell above the door chimes and a group of teenagers piles in. Resting my hand on Liv's arm, I smile and nod, moving away and hoping she gets my silent message that I got this.

Despite the butterflies in my chest, my award-winning smile plants itself on my face as I round the counter. "Hi there. How can I help you today?"

While I take the order, I can't help but continue to glance over at the happy family in the middle of the café.

My smile falters as I see something that feels like it may never happen for me.

Chapter 4

Zach

Being a cop in a small town is kind of...boring. I suppose it's better than the alternative of there being a lot of crime in Juniper Grove, though.

This time of year, with tourists being minimal, there aren't even many speeders.

I spend most of the time in my patrol car anyway, driving through the streets and watching at the speed traps.

"Officer Benning." The voice comes over my radio.

"Officer Benning here."

"We got a call from the pharmacy about Mrs. Henderson again."

"On it."

Dispatch doesn't need to say more. This is at least a monthly occurrence and has been for the past several years.

Pulling out of my spot, I head straight to the pharmacy. The only reason they even called me is that I've become somewhat of the Mrs. Henderson whisperer over the years, and I'm able to get her to calm down quickly and leave without a fuss.

The poor woman is in her nineties, so she just needs a gentle hand. And sometimes somebody to talk to.

I park in front of the store, leaving the lights on as I walk in. Mrs. Henderson can be heard screaming through the space.

It's a constant complaint. She thinks the store is stealing from her. That the medicine she's being given is fake and they just want her money. The poor woman has about a dozen prescriptions, so it's possible she's not entirely wrong, but I'd blame her doctor more than the pharmacy.

The fact that a woman of her age can project her voice to such an extreme is kind of impressive. Though, Mrs. Henderson is quite spritely for a woman in her nineties.

Her words are clearer to make out once I get closer. "That's my money you're taking! It's mine, and I want it back!"

"I'm sorry, Mrs. Henderson, but you're paying for your medication."

She throws a bottle of pills at the pharmacist. "Take them. I don't want them. I want my damn money."

I take a step forward and put my hand on hers. "Hello, Mary. How are you today?"

She turns to me with rage in her green eyes, but it calms as soon as she registers it's me. We've built a bond over the years of my responding to these calls. "Oh, Zachary. Good, you're here. Can you help me, please? They're stealing my money."

"Mary, we've talked about this. Dr. Pletha has prescribed you these medications because they're helping you live comfortably. If you don't take them, you could end up in the hospital or worse. We'd hate to lose you."

"But they're just so expensive." She slouches, a frown pulling at her brow with defeat.

"I know. And that's frustrating. But do you have to take it out on Wendy over there? She's just doing her job." I extend my hand toward the cowering brunette. What she's so afraid of, I have no idea. Sure, Mrs. Henderson threw a pill bottle, but it's not like she's going to jump over the counter at her. Probably.

"I'm sorry, young lady. I'm quite frustrated by this situation, and you are the one who is giving me the pills and taking the money."

"I think a few phone calls to the medication companies may make you feel better. You can yell at them all you like." I raise an eyebrow at my suggestion. This usually entices her to leave.

"That sounds lovely."

I extend my arm for her to take, and she wraps her wrinkled hands around it. We walk slowly out of the pharmacy and to my squad car.

"Let me drive you home, Mary."

"Nonsense, it's only two blocks away. I can walk." She straightens as she talks. Despite her age, she still walks through town and speed walks as her form of exercise. Sometimes I'm convinced the old broad is going to outlive all of us.

"I know you can, but I'd feel better if you let me give you a lift." We stand in a staring contest, and I know she's not going to give in unless I pull out the big guns. "Please? For me." I rest my fingers against my chest and give her my best puppy dog eyes.

She has to look up at me, as my six-foot-two frame towers over her, but I see the moment she relents as her whole body loosens. "Alright, Zachary. I'll let you give me a ride home."

One thing that can't be said about Mrs. Henderson is that she's losing her mind. She's sharp as a tack.

Resting her hand in mine, she lets me help her lower herself into the front seat, and I shut the door once she's safely inside.

At one point, Mrs. Henderson struck me as the kind that would *steal* a cop car if given the opportunity.

"What do you think, Mary? Lights or no lights?"

A wicked smile creeps across her face. "Siren and everything, Zachary."

"You got it, ma'am." With a smirk, I flick the lever to turn on the sirens, keeping the lights swirling.

Instead of going straight to Mrs. Henderson's, I make a few passes around the block. She lives close by, and I want to give her a nice joyride.

I'm sure if Mazie's in the café today she'll see us driving by. She knows I have a tendency to indulge Mrs. Henderson and that I'm the one on call. And the girls get some entertainment out of seeing the response to her tantrums.

It's been about ten minutes since we left the pharmacy, and Mrs. Henderson has a wide smile on her face, her eyes glinting in the sun as I pull into her driveway.

I look up at the modest house, knowing it's far too big for just her but she'll never move. The woman is going to die in that house, and probably haunt the new residents for decades to come.

Her house is practically an institution of Juniper Grove. One of the original houses left in town, it has been in her family for generations. Her late husband was in construction and did a lot of work to make it what it looks like today. They raised their four kids in that house, and while none of them have come back to Juniper Grove, I hope one of them will make the sacrifice to keep the residence in the family.

"Thank you, Zachary."

"As always, it's been a pleasure. But maybe next time, try not to get into it with the pharmacist."

She pushes her shoulders back. It's the same conversation every time. "I'll try better to contain my frustration. Please apologize again to

Wendy." Without giving me a chance to ensure I will, she's out of the car and walking up to the front door of her home.

I shake my head as I watch her disappear inside.

Well, at least that provided some entertainment to my day.

Chapter 5
Mazie

A lina has officially returned from her honeymoon, and I couldn't be happier to have her back. She's absolutely glowing and smiling more than I've seen in years.

But it also means I can seek the solace of my home once again. My therapist thinks it was good for me to get some extra time out and at the café, that it's necessary for me to learn to rebuild the trust in strangers, and being in what should be a safe place for me is the best way to do that.

She's right, but that doesn't mean I feel like opening myself up for that. A stranger killed my parents. Absolutely ripped them from our lives and changed my entire trajectory. Regardless of what my therapist thinks, I've sought safety in my house in the two weeks Alina's been back. But today I have to head back to the café to do inventory.

It's something I try to make sure I'm doing at least once a month, more frequently in busy months. Those touristy times, which are mostly summer and fall, keep us going. Our town draws a bigger crowd in the fall as the leaves change, especially with the nearby orchards, but we also have regular festivals. Enough that people will travel for them.

It helps that there's a small, private lake just on the town limits for a warm summer day. I used to frequent the lake in high school, but not for swimming.

We mostly stopped going after Mom and Dad died. The memories were just too painful. They used to take us there for a nice beach day in the summer. The one year Eli and I tried to get them to go, it ended with us three girls in tears, Liv storming into her room, and Eli drinking a beer on the back deck while he grilled some hamburgers for dinner.

Even though I stay home most days, I get myself fully dressed each morning. Today was a hair washing day, so my curls fall in auburn curtains over my shoulders. One final glance in the mirror by the front door and a deep breath has me heading out.

Adjusting my purse strap on my shoulder, I lock the front door, then check that it's locked. I bound down the front steps before climbing back up them to check one more time that the door is, in fact, locked.

Fully satisfied, I walk back down the steps and get into my car. Though Juniper Grove isn't very big, and I could probably walk to the café, I feel better being locked inside my car. You'd think with my parents being murdered in a carjacking gone wrong, I wouldn't want to ever step foot in a car again, but it beats being out in the open. At five-foot-three, I'd be easy to grab, lift, and drag away.

The thought alone makes me shudder, and my hand slides into my purse for my phone, which I clutch in my fist.

Zach's always only a call away. Any time of day or night. And not just because he *is* 911. He's made it exceptionally clear that I can call him any time, even if I'm just feeling uneasy, which he knows is most of the time.

He's certainly been over a few dozen times when I heard something suspicious in the middle of the night. There's never been anything of concern, but he doesn't complain, even offering to stay in case the sound returns. I always feel bad and tell him it's okay and often don't get much more sleep until the sun is up.

Things are less scary in the daylight.

Shaking my head, I get back on track. I have things to do at the café today and want to be sure I'm not there any longer than necessary.

I park behind Liv's BMW. Ever since she moved to the freaking mansion on the hill, she's too far away to walk, more on the cusp of town than the center.

"Hey, Zee. Did we know you were coming by today?" She always thinks I have some ulterior motive for being here. That I can't just want to see them or get some work done. It's probably because I'm not here often.

"Inventory day."

"Ah." She nods and runs a rag over the counter. Though perhaps a bit unorthodox in both her dress and demeanor, she makes a good front of house. She likes to keep it neat and tidy, cleaning regularly, and though there can be snark to her, she's friendly and outgoing.

She gets that from Dad.

Walking around the counter, I rest a hand on her shoulder as I head back to my closet office. I toss my purse onto the desk and turn to the filing cabinet. I keep separate lists for what we need for each part of the cafe. Things for Alina we tend to need to order more frequently than cups and lids for Liv.

The clipboard hangs on a hook on the back of the door, and I pull it off with a swift movement, snagging a pen from my desk and heading straight to the kitchen.

Alina's elbow deep in batter, with flour in her chocolate curls. I'm not sure she's ever here without flour somewhere on her person. And usually that same set of curls is what's caked in the stuff.

"Hey, Leen." I grab a raspberry off the counter in front of her and pop it in my mouth. A sweet, floral deliciousness fills my mouth.

"Hey, Maze. What brings you in today?" She mixes the bowl of whatever's in front of her and huffs some hair from her face. Though she wears it pulled back, a few strands always fall loose. In fact, the more strands and spots of flour on her forehead, the harder she's been working.

"Inventory. I'm going to start in here, if that's okay?"

"Sure."

"What are you making?" Curiosity gets the better of me. I usually don't ask because it doesn't matter, as anything she whips up is incredible. And I'm just happy to have her back. Now we can stop buying pastries from elsewhere and our regulars will be happy.

"Mixed berry muffins. Liv's favorite."

I wonder if she'd make my favorite if she knew I was going to be in. I wonder if she even knows what it is. Cinnamon crunch.

There's a lot that I keep to myself because I don't want to be too vulnerable with them. While they get to be just sisters, I have to keep that motherly role about myself. Though they're not the young girls they were when I took over the parenting, they're still my baby sisters.

"Can't wait. So, tell me, what are you running low on?" I hold the clipboard, ready to scribble as she tends to ramble things off in quick succession.

"Flour, sugar, molasses, chocolate powder, baking soda, baking powder, eggs, always eggs, milk, butter. More muffin wrappers, we need brioche for the sandwiches, more hard rolls, lettuce, cheddar, Swiss, turkey, rye bread. Hm. I'm sure there's more."

I give her a second as I catch up writing everything down, my head bobbing as I try to remember it all.

"Oh! More paper for wrapping the sandwiches. And whatever fresh fruit you can get me."

"Do you need any more of the jarred or canned stuff?"

She wrinkles her nose as she looks at me. "Nope. I try to use that as sparingly as possible. And since it's spring, it should be getting into prime season."

"Alright. What about the farmer's market? Doesn't that start again soon?" Late spring through early fall, there tends to be a farmer's market just around the corner.

"Yeah, in a few weeks. I already have all the dates on my calendar." Alina is picky about the fresh ingredients she uses. Even though she encouraged me to get her some, she'll still pick through it for the best parts.

A few years ago, after we got into a major fight about how much she wastes from what I order, I encouraged her to seek out the farmer's market and pick up what she can on the company credit card.

It helps keep our costs lower when it's going because, while it may be slightly more expensive, we throw away far less. It also allows her to make some seasonal favorites. She did something with some fresh plums last year that was to die for.

As I'm checking the piles of to-go boxes and containers, my phone vibrates in my pocket.

Zach: *I'm off Friday. Movie night?*

A smile spans my face.

Me: *Of course. Whose turn is it?*

We have a long-standing tradition of movie nights on any Friday that Zach doesn't have to work. Sometimes that's three in a row, sometimes it's not for six weeks.

Zach: *I'm pretty sure it's mine.*

My eyes narrow, and I groan internally. He always picks scary movies, even though I don't like them. More than once, he's had to spend the night so that I could get some semblance of sleep. Most of the time, I watch the movie from between my fingers or behind a pillow.

And every time, Zach laughs at me. Yet he can't seem to be bothered to pick a different genre.

Me: *Ugh. Fine. What scary thing are you going to make me watch this time.*

Zach: *You'll see ;)*

Oh, great. A surprise so I can't even look it up first.

"Tell Zach I say hi," Alina sing-songs as I slide the phone back into my pocket.

"How did you know I was talking to Zach?"

She points her mixing spoon at me, batter dripping onto the counter. Her food may be delicious, but she's a hot mess in the kitchen. "Because you only get that dopey smile on your face when you talk to him."

"I do not get a dopey smile." There's little conviction to my tone as my cheeks heat. Zach has always brought out a certain reaction from me. He's gorgeous and kind, muscular and sweet, tall and protective. What part isn't meant to get the heart racing?

But we're just friends. I'd always been his best friend's little sister, but then at a certain point, we all started hanging out together. Then when Eli left for MIT and Zach stayed behind, we became even closer, a dynamic duo. It was rare then to find one of us without the other.

"For one, you definitely do. I don't know what your hesitation is, Mazie. You two are clearly into each other and have been for years."

"We're just friends. Sure, we're really close, but it ends at friendship."

She rolls her eyes and sighs heavily. "Whatever you say."

I chew on my lip and watch her spoon the batter into the muffin tins. She and Liv are always giving me a hard time that there's more between me and Zach. And I always shrug them off. But then at the wedding, there seemed like there was something he wanted to tell me and wouldn't. Or couldn't.

I shake the thought away. No use getting my hopes up over nothing.

Chapter 6
Zach

Movie nights are one of my favorite things. Not only do I get to relax and watch a great film, but I get to spend time with Mazie. The fact that she spends half of them as a terrified little ball in the corner of the couch is just an added perk.

Poking fun at each other is a long-standing tradition. As is making her watch scary movies. She makes me watch that romantic shit on her nights, so it's only fair. Besides, there's a method to my madness, even if it hasn't worked yet.

One day, one day it will.

And until then, I'll keep finding scary movies to watch. At least I also bring snacks. Mazie's favorite is Twizzlers, while I prefer Raisinets. She'll always have her feet pulled up under her while she sinks into the corner and half hides behind a pillow, chewing one candy at a time while I just dump the box back and catch whatever falls in my mouth.

Tonight's no exception, as I walk up to the door holding our snacks and knowing exactly what movie to pick from her streaming services. She answers the door after I knock, her curls loose and hanging over her shoulders. All the air leaves my lungs. She's utterly breathtaking, even in comfy pants and a t-shirt.

"Hey." She's breathless, as though she ran to answer the door.

"Were you not expecting me?" I glance at my watch. Eight o'clock, like always.

"I was. I was just cleaning up a bit." She steps aside and extends her arm, inviting me in.

Right away, I take my shoes off, per Mazie protocol. She's so strict about it that the sisters have the same rules. Eli could care less, but I notice him taking his shoes off as soon as he walks through the door, so I usually do too.

I'm pretty sure it's just ingrained from her mother. We always had to take our shoes off as kids. It made sense then, as they were often muddy or covered in some foreign substance, like most kids' shoes are. Mazie has gone to great lengths to keep the memory of Jenna alive in as many ways as she can, and keeping the shoe rule is a simple one.

Without words, I extend the Twizzler bag to Mazie, which she quickly grabs and tears open, taking one out and biting into it. I take a look around the house. I'm sure whatever mess she was referring to is imaginary since she keeps her home spotless. I could show up at any given moment and it'd be neat as a pin.

I flop down on the couch, putting my feet up on the table. It earns a scowl from Mazie, but she doesn't say anything and settles into her corner.

The sofa is small, so we're not terribly far apart, but we're not touching either. I wouldn't mind her being a little closer.

But how do you tell your best friend that your feelings go beyond friendship? You don't. Or at least, I won't. If this friendship and time together is all we ever have, it's better than risking it by telling her I have feelings for her and her not reciprocating and then feeling weird around me.

I grab the remote from the table and navigate my way to the proper channel and select the movie. Turning to Mazie with a raised eyebrow, I already find her halfway huddled behind a pillow, and chuckle lightly to myself. "You ready for this?"

"As ready as I ever am." So not really, but she's willing to be a good sport for me.

I settle into the couch, tearing open my box of Raisinets and tipping it back. The chocolatey chewy goodness fills my mouth.

When the introduction credits come on a bit loudly, Mazie jumps, and I can't help but smile and laugh lightly to myself.

"What are you so scared of? You know it's fake."

"It doesn't feel like it while watching it. My heart is racing."

"That's exactly what there is to love about them. A little scare, a little adrenaline."

"I'll pass. But I'm willing to watch for you." She turns and looks at me with a glimmer in her eyes.

Now I feel guilty. Before we even started movie night, I made sure the scary ones wouldn't trigger anything for her and the murder of her parents. She assured me it wouldn't, but suddenly I'm not so sure.

Reaching forward, I grab the remote from where I left it on the table and pause the movie.

"Are you really okay watching this? I can find something else."

"It's not my favorite genre of movie, but it is yours. You suffer for me." She picks at the frill on the pillow in her lap.

"Yeah, but yours don't scare me. They just don't entertain me."

"It's not a big deal. Really. They just cause nightmares. Like that one with the aliens." She shudders as if remembering.

"They're not triggering anything about your parents?"

She winces slightly at the word. It's something I've never shied away from. Especially since she told me that her therapist said she needed to use and hear the word more frequently. I guess it's part of her healing journey.

Not a single one of the Bakers came out unscathed. Even Liv who was a preteen at the time. But Mazie took a large portion on herself. Not only did she lose her parents and step into that mother role right away, but I'm pretty sure she never truly grieved the loss.

I'm fairly certain she went right from learning of the loss and being a sister, straight into mom mode. And I'm not sure she ever really stepped out.

"No, they're not triggering. You're good about not picking slasher films, just scary things." It's true. I avoid choosing anything that would qualify as a slasher and stick to things that are just plain creepy.

"You know, if they ever are—"

"I can tell you. I know." She rests her fingers on my forearm and sparks ignite beneath the surface of my skin. "I can always talk to you about anything and be honest with you. I know that." There's sincerity in her eyes and she says it like it's the surest thing she's ever known.

Before I can stop myself, something takes over me, and I lace my fingers through hers. She inhales sharply. It's not like we've never held hands before, but there's something about this moment that makes it more intimate.

Which is why when I notice her parted lips, I lean forward, slowly and slightly. I only make it about halfway before I pause, not sure if I should continue but fighting everything inside me that wants to press my lips to hers.

When her breath caresses against my face, when she *doesn't* back away, I'm done in. Heart pounding, I bring my free hand up to cup the back of her head, running my nose along her jaw before brushing my lips against hers.

Fireworks explode within me. I've been waiting for this for so long.

Just a small taste isn't enough. I tighten my hold on the back of her head and press my mouth firmly against hers, slipping my tongue along the seam of her lips. With a moan, she parts them, and my tongue dives into her mouth. I'm not usually a fan of spearmint albeit mixed with the sugary sweetness of the Twizzlers, but now it's my favorite flavor.

She separates her hand from mine and plants both on my chest. For a second, I'm worried she's going to push me away, but instead she fists my shirt and pulls me closer.

I grip her around the waist and pull her into my lap, keeping my mouth moving against hers. Her curls cascade around us. Losing my fingers in the hair at her nape, I tighten them into a fist, and she whimpers into my mouth and grinds her hips against mine.

Fuck, she's so much sexier than I ever let myself realize.

One of my hands glides down her back and plants firmly into her back pocket, pulling her closer.

I'm able to give her ass one squeeze before her palms flatten against my chest and she pulls her mouth from mine, her chest heaving.

"What are we doing?" Her forehead falls onto my collarbone, but she doesn't move away.

I twirl a curl around my finger and pull it straight down her spine. "Haven't you ever thought about it, M? Us?"

The moment she hesitates and swallows thickly, I know this isn't going to go the way I want it to. She lowers herself so she's sitting on my knees and her gaze meets mine.

I've memorized every sparkle and freckle of those brilliant sapphire eyes, but I also see they're filled with something along the lines of remorse.

"You're my best friend, Zach." Ouch.

Subtly, I shift beneath her and remove my hand from her back pocket. It doesn't feel appropriate anymore. "Is that it, though? Is that all we are?"

Her chin drops to her chest. "I'm not willing to risk losing you. I need you in my life, and if we tried something and it didn't work, I don't think we'd be able to stay friends."

A heavy sigh deflates my chest, and I drop my hands to my sides. "I should go." I shift to get up, and she scrambles off my lap and stands.

"Wait, no. Don't go. Let's watch our movie." She wraps her fingers around my forearm, but I pull out of her grasp.

"I don't want to anymore, Mazie." Grabbing my lightweight coat from one of her kitchen chairs, I head straight for the front door. "I'll...see you later. I just can't be here right now." I don't even turn to look at her as I slam the door shut behind me.

The cool night air puffs in front of my face as I exhale and shove my hands into my pockets.

Home is the last place I want to go. With a sigh, I amble down the front steps and get into my car, taking one look back at the house. Mazie's standing in the window, holding on to the curtain. One hand raises in a slight wave, and her fingertips rest against the window. The most I can give her is a nod.

I head to the only place I can think of. Though he's surely going to call me an idiot.

Chapter 7
Mazie

What just happened? How did the night turn so abruptly?

My lips are still tingling, and my heart is still racing from that kiss. Who would have guessed Zach is such a good kisser. I mean, my God. My fingers graze along my mouth, remembering the pressure of his lips.

But they fall when I remember he's my best friend. I can't risk losing that bond, that connection. Relationships never go right for me. I always fuck them up or they can't handle my oddities and obsessive compulsions.

That can't happen between me and Zach, because I *need* him in my life. And I wouldn't be able to go back to being just friends with him. Especially not after a kiss like that. I can only imagine what else he can do with that tongue.

I can't honestly say that I've never thought about it. In fact, when I was younger, before he and I became as close as we are, I used to dream about being his girlfriend. He's always been a looker, with that dirty blond hair, those piercing green eyes, and toned body. Back in high school, I fawned over him.

But then everything changed. *Life* changed. He was there for me during the hardest part of my life, when I lost my parents and had to become somebody my siblings could rely on. I had to be strong, while letting them be weak. Zach became my safe space. My space to have my breakdowns, to get my emotions out without my sisters seeing. Eli knew I was bottling it all up. He kept telling me it wasn't healthy, but I felt like I had no choice.

Has Zach been thinking about this for a while? Nothing has ever been different in his demeanor or our exchanges. What was his end goal?

Zach's not really the premeditative type. I don't think he came over tonight planning to make a move. It just sort of...happened. When he leaned in, it's like I was stuck in place and couldn't pull away. I didn't want to.

Even still, where did his mind go? He asked if I've ever thought about us, but does he mean as part of a relationship? Or just friends with benefits?

No, it doesn't matter. We can't cross that line.

Grabbing my phone from the entry table, I send a quick SOS text to Liv and Alina. I know they have their own lives—Liv has a baby, for fuck's sake—but this is important.

My phone pings back in rapid succession that they're both on their way. Which means I can confidently pace the house while I await their arrival.

That's one thing I love about having my sisters so close. It's part of the trauma we went through. We rally around each other without question.

Alina's the first to burst through the door. She takes one look at me pacing, chewing on my cuticles, and walks right over to me and puts her hands on my shoulders. Her eyes track over my face, looking for something. Some giveaway of what happened and why I messaged them.

Liv comes barreling through the door next, kicking off her shoes, and coming right up to where Alina and I are standing in the middle of my house.

"What is it? What's wrong?" There's a touch of panic in Liv's voice. Ever since she became a mom, she's been a lot more concerned about the rest of us, not needing to be babied anymore, but often doing the babying.

Pulling my lip between my teeth, I wring my fingers as I look between both of them.

"Zach kissed me."

Their shoulders noticeably slump, and they look at one another for an intense moment before smiling and looking back at me.

But I don't like the look they just exchanged, and my eyes narrow. "What? What is it? You know something."

"How long have we been saying that Zach's in love with you, Zee?" Liv cocks her head to the side as she asks.

"Yeah, but you guys are crazy. Picking up on things that aren't there."

"Or maybe you're the one who's been blind this whole time. I mean, come on, Mazie, there has to be something that we see that you don't." Alina sounds frustrated with me, which is unlike her.

Though, they have been telling me for ages. I always thought it got into one of their heads and then they planted the seed in the other. I wonder if Eli's in on this thought process too.

"But...why wouldn't he say anything?"

"Probably for the same reason you texted us. You're scared and don't know what to do now." Liv's perception is something I've always been jealous of.

"Well, what *do* I do now? I told him I couldn't."

"What do you want to do?"

I walk away from them and flop onto the couch, resting my elbows on my knees and hiding my face in my hands. "I don't know."

"Come on, Maze. You've really never thought about it before?" The couch dips next to me as Alina sits and puts a hand on my back.

The couch dips on the other side a moment later.

"Honestly? I think I've tried to keep my mind from ever going there. He's been such a source of comfort for me, I wouldn't risk ruining that."

"What makes you think you'd ruin it?"

"The fact that not a single relationship has ever lasted beyond a few months."

"But he already knows you. He knows your idiosyncrasies and quirks and still hangs around. He's less likely to leave because of them."

I can't decide if it's a good thing or bad thing that Liv knows why my past relationships haven't lasted.

"That doesn't mean he wants to take them on full time."

"You're not as hard to handle as you think you are, Mazie." Alina runs her hand down my back, trying to soothe me.

That may be so, but that doesn't mean I need to be anybody's burden. I haven't been since the second my parents died. I won't become one now.

"The two of you certainly think I'm a bit much." I look between the two of them and catch the way their eyes lock on one another's.

"It's different, Mazie. You're our sister and often act like our mother, which neither of us really needs anymore."

"And don't you think as a significant other, it could be too much?"

"I don't know. It's a different dynamic than siblings. But Zach is used to you. And if he loves you, like we're all pretty sure he does, then he fell in love with you despite those things."

"And let's be honest. You could certainly do worse than Zach. He's sweet and caring and strong. He'd protect the hell out of you, which I know is a fear of yours." Liv tucks a curl behind my ear.

How did my baby sisters end up comforting me? I asked them to come more to talk the nonsense out of me, but instead they're taking care of me.

The roles don't often reverse for us, and I'm not sure how to feel about it. A little out of control, at least.

"The only thing you have to decide now is if you want to take it to the next level or keep things the way they are." Alina's voice is calming.

"What happened when you told him you couldn't?"

My eyes meet Liv's and they're that soft shade of purple. "He left."

"Maybe give him a few days to cool down and then touch base. It gives you time to think about what you want too."

I nod relentlessly. That sounds good.

Now the only question is, what do I want?

Chapter 8
Zach

I bounce on the balls of my feet as I knock on Eli's door. The second he answers, his eyes widen for a moment before he steps aside and holds his arm out, welcoming me into his apartment.

He's got a baseball game on and a beer on the table. Thankfully, it doesn't look like I interrupted much.

"What's up? Wasn't expecting you tonight." He flops back into his recliner and grabs his beer from the table, taking a swig.

"I kissed Mazie."

And he promptly spews beer all over his living room table and practically chokes on the sip. "You did *what*?"

I run a hand through my hair and tug at the roots as the other plants on my hip. I haven't even taken my jacket off, let alone sit down. "It just sort of...happened. It was movie night, and we were talking about how if my scary choices triggered anything for her, we didn't have to watch them, and she was just so sincere, and I don't know what I was thinking."

"I do."

My eyes flick over to his, and I see amusement bouncing through his irises. "You're in love with my sister. You have been for years."

I take a step back at his declaration. "That's crazy. We're best friends."

He lifts one shoulder as he leans forward, his hands between his knees as he pulls at the label of the beer bottle. "Doesn't change the fact that you're in love with her."

"Does that...does that piss you off?" Aren't brothers supposed to hate their friends and sisters being together?

His eyes raise to meet mine. "At one point, it might have. It did...actually. I could tell you had feelings for her, and though you didn't act on them, I knew, and it irritated the crap out of me. She's my sister. I hate to think of *anybody* being with my sisters. But two of them are married now, one has a kid, and we're all adults. It's the reality of life. I've come to accept it." He takes another sip of his beer. "Plus, better you than some schmuck off the street."

I don't know if that should make me feel better or worse.

"So, what exactly happened?"

"Are you sure you want to hear this?"

"No, but I'm also your friend," he pauses and tips his bottle in my direction, "and that's what you need right now, so I can try to turn off big brother mode for the moment."

I'm going to choose to trust him in this instance. Worst case, I end up with a black eye. "I was over at Mazie's for movie night. It was my choice to pick, so naturally I went with a scary movie."

"Naturally."

"And as you probably know, your sister hates scary movies, but she makes me watch those damn romcoms, and she's always said she's okay with it. So, when she was hiding, I wanted to check in and make sure it wasn't triggering any bad memories or anything related to...you know…your parents." I never quite know how to bring it up to any of them.

He stiffens but doesn't say anything.

"She assured me that it wasn't, and that she knew she could tell me, and it was just the way she laid her hand on my arm, the sureness and trust in her eyes. I just…I leaned forward, and she didn't move away, and then I was kissing her. And things got a little heated before she pushed me away and asked what we were doing."

"And what were you doing?"

I raise an eyebrow as I fall to the couch. "Is this where we get into the 'what are your intentions with my sister' conversation?"

"Not really. You're a good guy and my friend, and I trust you not to hurt Mazie. But be careful. She can be…a lot to handle. Which I'm sure you already know."

Irritation flutters through my veins. "I don't know why you all say that. She's not a lot to handle. Sure, she has some personality quirks and things that can be frustrating, but it's understandable with what you've all been through."

"That right there makes you better than any guy she's ever tried to be with before."

My jaw ticks. Though we've both dated over the years, I've never really felt a strong connection with any of the women I've pursued. And while I've never really faced it head on, I like to think that's the reason nothing has ever worked out for Mazie.

The kiss shifted things. There's now varying shades and hues to our relationship, and it's making my head spin as I work back through memories.

I've never liked the guys she's dated, never felt like they were good enough for her. I chalked it up to being good friends and always left it at that.

Now I know there's always been more to it.

How stupid am I?

I lean back into the couch and stare up at the ceiling. "What am I doing?"

"I don't know. What do you want to do?"

"I wish I knew."

"Think about it for a minute. I have nowhere to be." His chair creaks as he leans back.

There really isn't much to think about. The answer feels like it's been staring me in the face for weeks now, if not longer. The problem is that I don't know how to go about getting what I want.

"I want to be with Mazie. Fuck, how am I just now realizing this?"

"You're not. It's just the first time you've had the thought sober."

I shoot straight up, and my hands fall to my knees as my eyes narrow. "What do you mean by that?"

His brows shoot up on his forehead, and he freezes with the bottle halfway to his mouth. "Shit."

"That doesn't make anything better. What the fuck are you talking about?"

"How much do you remember from Alina's wedding?"

Thinking for a moment, I wrack my brain to pull up something, anything. "Not really a lot. I got overly intoxicated that night. After the ceremony and dinner, things get a little lost. Then, the next thing I remember is waking up at Mazie's. Which, thanks, by the way. I'm sure you had a hand in getting me back there." I'm not exactly sure where he's going with this and what Alina's wedding has to do with anything.

While I can usually hold my liquor far better, that night did get the best of me. Did I do something stupid?

"Well, part of what caught our attention was that you were adamant about how much you love Mazie and you just had to tell her. You don't remember that? I thought for sure you were just keeping quiet about it."

Fantastic. Just what I was hoping to hear. Ugh. I'd be more mortified if it wasn't Eli, and he hadn't seen me in far more embarrassing situations. "Nope. Don't remember a damn thing. Did she hear me?"

"No. Just me and Cam. We somehow intervened as you were on your way to tell her. I figured a drunken confession wasn't exactly what you were aiming for."

I slouch in my seat with a groan.

"For what it's worth, we've all known for years. The only ones who don't seem to realize the two of you are meant to be together, are the two of you."

"Even better." A heavy sigh pulls from my chest as I stare at a spider on the ceiling. Mazie would be terrified, and I'd have to kill it. She's not a fan of catching and releasing, thinking they'll come back for vengeance.

A thought occurs to me, and I lean forward, resting my elbows on my knees, eyes narrowed. "So, you all know? Like Liv and Alina and their husbands?"

Silently, he takes a sip of his beer as he nods.

My brows furrow. "Is it some sort of game to you all? Are we the butt of your family joke? Does Mazie not even realize that her family is making fun of her?"

Eli holds his hands up in peace. "Whoa, whoa, whoa. We don't make fun of you guys at all. We're just shocked you haven't gotten to this point yet. And there may be a pool for when you finally get together, but that's not important."

I'm on my feet, eyebrows high in a heartbeat. "A *pool?* Are you fucking serious?" I run a shaky hand through my hair and look around the room. It's suddenly stifling in here. "I gotta go. I can't stay here."

Without waiting for an answer, I head for the door, but hear Eli's chair snap back to position and know he's hot on my tail.

"Wait. Zach, just wait a minute damn it."

I freeze and turn toward him.

The way he stops walking and rolls his eyes, my face must be sending a clear message of distrust right now.

"What do you want me to say, Zach?"

"You're supposed to be my best friend. I want to know why you never brought this up before."

"And what exactly do you propose I say to you? 'Hey, asshole, I'm pretty sure you're in love with my sister but don't seem to notice it?'"

He's right, of course. There's really no way to bring up something like that.

"I don't know. But I don't like hearing that we're some sort of joke to you all."

"Not a joke. Never a joke. We love you both, and you're basically already a brother to us, minus the legality of it. We just don't understand how you've never realized your feelings before. Either one of you. Well...we understand Mazie. She's a stubborn one. And I'm kidding about the pool. Sort of." He shrugs a shoulder like it's no big deal instead of something life altering.

Though I need to leave, I don't know what the next step should be. "What do I do now?"

"Whatever you want. You *know* Mazie, probably better than anybody. Right now, she's likely just as confused as you are."

"That's not helpful."

He rubs a hand along the back of his neck. "Look. I'm obviously not well versed in the romance department, especially since all my younger siblings seem to be getting together before me and I haven't had a girlfriend in years. But just talk to her. Be honest. Or ignore it completely. Whichever you feel is best."

I look down as I shuffle my feet. What's best. I have no idea what that is in this situation. I don't even know how Mazie feels about it all.

For all I know, she's freaking out and planning to never invite me over again.

And while part of me is dying to find out, I'm not sure I could handle the rejection.

With no more than a nod, I walk out Eli's front door.

Once in the car, I bang my head against the steering wheel a few times. I'm not sure where I'm going, or what I'm doing, but right now, the dark night is my only companion.

Chapter 9
Mazie

It's been almost two weeks since I've talked to Zach, which is highly unusual. Even if our schedules don't align to see each other at least once, which is a rarity, we usually text a few times a day. Not hearing from him makes me uncomfortable in my own skin. It's such a part of my day that I'm off without it.

And while I've certainly clicked on his name, my fingers hovering above the keys, I have no idea what to say to him. I'm assuming it's the reason I have yet to hear from him.

That, or he quickly realized that kissing me was a mistake, and now he doesn't know how to move forward. It's the most likely scenario.

I bide my time by not sleeping, pacing the house, and driving my sisters crazy by being a presence at the shop. Normally, I work from home. But I keep replaying the night over and over in my mind. I swear his woodsy cologne still lingers in the air.

Being in my own house has never driven me so crazy. It's always been my comfort location, yet now I can barely stand being here.

All because of a kiss.

Well, maybe not entirely just the kiss. There are these thoughts, dreams, daydreams that haunt me every moment of the day. What if it had gone further? What if I hadn't stopped him? I'm going to eventually see him again. It's inevitable. What happens then? My thoughts go from tame to anything but. It's hard to rein them in. And it's even harder to differentiate which I prefer.

The days have both dragged by and blended together into one jumbled mess. When you own a business that's open seven days a week, it's easy for everything to meld into one.

In fact, it's not until my doorbell rings at eight o'clock that I even realize it's Friday. But...it can't be.

And yet, when the door swings open, there stands Zach, holding a six-pack, a bag of microwavable popcorn, and two packs of candy, including my Twizzlers.

"Um. Hi?" It comes out almost like a question. But since I haven't heard from him in two weeks, I wasn't exactly expecting him.

Instead of giving me much of an answer, he lifts one shoulder. "It's movie night."

I have to shake away the haze I find myself under and move to the side to let him in. I'm practically clinging to the door, needing to keep my balance. "Come on in."

A strong burst of his scent infiltrates my senses as he brushes past me and makes his way into the living room. He walks through the house and settles on the couch as though he lives here, making himself right at home.

I'm a little too stunned by the fact that he showed up unannounced to even put words together. So instead, I close and lock the door, twisting and untwisting the lock three times...just to be sure.

"Hey." I look up at the deep tenor of his voice. "You don't have to do that when I'm here." He points to his chest. "Cop. Remember? I'll keep you safe." The sincerity that sweeps through his eyes is enough to make my breath halt.

Heat creeps into my cheeks. "It just makes me feel better." I never knew he noticed.

"I know. And that's fine. But you don't have to when I'm around. Just saying." He's not forceful about it. The way his words come across is as though he's sharing a thought that maybe I've never had before.

"Thank you." While that seems incredibly stupid to say, how does one respond to that?

I pull the cuffs of my sleeves into my hands and take a moment to look at my attire. I wasn't expecting anybody, least of all Zach, and am donned in an oversized long-sleeved tee and a pair of pajama shorts, which I give a quick tug down so they're not showing off my ass quite as much.

"You gonna come sit? I brought your Twizzlers. I know not to dare enter the house for movie night without them." He looks over at me from his spot on the couch with raised eyebrows and waggles the bag of Twizzlers at me.

"Oh. Um. Of course. Sorry. I just wasn't expecting you is all." I practically skip across the room to the couch and tuck a stray curl behind my ear before flopping down in my usual seat at the end. Most of my hair is piled in a messy ponytail, but there's a few dangling strands.

Zach silently passes me the Twizzlers, which I promptly tear open, and I take a big bite of one. I don't know what to say, so I'd rather make my mouth busy chewing.

"I know we haven't talked in a few days. Sorry about that. I just, uh, wanted to give you some space. I guess. But every Friday I'm free is movie night. And I'm off tonight, so I figured I'd chance coming over and let you tell me to get lost."

"I'd never tell you to get lost, Zach." While I'm not exactly sure where things stand, for him or myself, he's still my best friend. I hope.

I curl my feet up under me and sit completely straight and stiff. I've never been so nervous around him, and I have no idea what to do with myself. Which is ridiculous because we know each other so well.

Am I going to let a little kiss derail our relationship?

No fucking way.

Pushing my shoulders back a bit more, I tip my chin up and lean back against the couch. "So, what are we watching? My turn, right?" I lean forward to reach for the remote, but he beats me to it, waving it in my face.

"Uh, uh. Not so fast. We didn't get to watch my movie last time, so I get a redo."

My jaw drops. "Are you serious? You're going to make me watch *another* scary movie?" The audacity.

"It's only fair. We didn't get to watch the whole movie, not even half of it."

I settle further into the cushion and pull a pillow into my lap, hugging it tightly to my chest. "I guess I'm ready then." Before pulling the pillow up to my chin, I grab another Twizzler and take a large bite.

Twizzlers have been my favorite movie snack for as long as I can remember. When I was younger, I used to bite off both ends and pretend it was a straw, through which I would drink from my can of soda, usually Sprite.

As Zach works his way through the TV to find the right streaming service for the movie he wants, I chance a glance out of the corner of my eye.

Has he always been so attractive? I mean, I certainly have noticed. I'd have to be blind not to. But has he always been *this* devastatingly handsome? Maybe it's something about the way his hair is styled tonight, where a few strands are hanging across his forehead. Or maybe it's the shirt. It's tight across his chest and at his arms, in literally all the right places.

But then again, he's jacked. His shirts are *always* tight. Maybe it's the color. It's a shade of teal that brings out the green in his eyes.

It's not until one corner of his mouth ticks up that I know he notices me staring. With a quick clear of my throat, I turn away, thoroughly mortified.

What is wrong with me? One kiss, and now I can't stop staring at him like some lovesick puppy?

And the way he came here and walked in so nonchalantly, it's clear that he just wants to move on and pretend that nothing happened. He needed the two weeks to clear his head, to let the air settle between us. But he doesn't want anything to come from it.

Which is fine. I can put it out of my head. I think. It's been driving me crazy for two weeks, but I can let it go.

And I'm doing a fine job of that as the movie starts, and I half hide behind my pillow. Until Zach's hand lands firmly on my thigh. My head snaps sideways to look at him, but he's focused on the screen.

He must notice me looking at him, though, because he gives my leg a squeeze.

With a quick huff, I reach to the table and pause the movie, thanking the heavens above that it's not a scary scene. I sit cross-legged and turn to face him, hands falling into my lap.

"Okay. What are you doing?"

He turns to look at me with a raised eyebrow. "Trying to watch a movie. Isn't that what we do on movie night? Well, maybe not you since you hide behind a pillow through basically the whole thing, but you get the idea."

"You know that's not what I mean, Zachary." It's rare that I use his full name, but I need him to know that I'm being serious right now.

Instead of the straight answer I'm hoping for, the corners of his lips turn up in a wicked grin. "Why don't you tell me *exactly* what you mean then."

Fuck. He's going to make this difficult isn't he. "You kissed me. And then I haven't heard from you in *two weeks* and suddenly you show up on my door like nothing has happened and no time has passed."

"I was giving you some space."

"Space?"

"Yeah. To think about what happened. It's clear that you didn't want it to, based on what you said that night and seeing as I haven't heard a word from you since then either. So, I needed a little time to get myself right, to be sure I could put it past me and not let it affect our friendship. I'm at that point and it was a free Friday. Which is movie night." The way he says it all is so matter-of-fact, except he got one thing wrong.

"I never said that I didn't want it to happen."

His eyebrows shoot to his hairline, and his mouth opens and closes like a fish. "I—uh—what?" He blinks repeatedly and turns his body to face me fully, utter confusion sprawled across his features.

"I never said I didn't want it to happen. It took me by surprise, sure. And at first, I didn't know what to make of it. But I've been able to digest it now, to put some thought into it."

"And?" Maybe it's just me, but it sounds like the single word is tinged with hope.

"And...I don't know. I honestly can't say where I stand because you were nowhere to be seen or heard from for two weeks." Exasperated, I throw my hands up before dropping them to my lap.

"What exactly did you expect me to say? Sorry I kissed you and you hated it? Let's just move on? You didn't say anything either."

"*You* kissed *me*. If anybody was expected to say something, it's you!" Honestly, I can't believe we're even arguing about who should have contacted who.

He runs his hand down his face, pulling his mouth open in the process. We sit in silence, staring at each other for a few moments, neither of us sure what to say.

"Oh, fuck this." Without warning, he reaches out and wraps his fingers around my wrist, tugging me into his lap and crashing his mouth to mine.

Looping an arm around me, he tips me backward as his tongue dives between my lips. His other hand cups my cheek and his thumb brushes under my eye.

My legs are over his lap, and I'm being held just above the couch cushions, having a tongue war with my best friend, when he suddenly stops and pulls away.

We're both breathing heavily, and he rests his forehead against mine, trailing the hand that was against my face down my arm and linking our fingers together.

"Do you want this, Mazie? With me? I'll be okay if you say no, we'll still be friends, but don't say yes if you don't mean it."

My answer is immediate. Like his touch has erased any questions or concerns from my mind. "Yes. I definitely do." The only thing I've wanted since that first kiss is *more*. More kisses, more passion, more Zach.

Instead of closing the gap and joining our mouths again, he hesitates, pulling back slightly so his eyes can meet mine. He's looking for any shred of doubt. But he won't find one.

"Really? I can take it if the answer is no."

I link my fingers behind his neck and smile. "Really." It comes out through a giggle.

"Thank fuck."

He lowers me so my back is flat against the cushions, and his lips lock on mine again. This time, they're hurried, frantic, like he's trying to make sure he gets everything in before I change my mind.

But that's not going to happen.

His hands trail down my body, giving my breasts a squeeze as he passes over them, pinching my nipples before he continues his track down my body.

After that first kiss, when I thought about this happening, when I wondered what it might be like to be *more* with Zach, never in a million years did I expect my body to zing the way it is now. I thought maybe it'd be strange or awkward, since we've been friends for so long and know each other on such a personal and intimate level.

Not a single ounce of this is awkward or strange or anything other than exactly right.

With a slight adjustment, he's hovering over me, his parted mouth gliding down my neck. He slides up the hem of my shirt and lays a path of kisses from the hem of my shorts up to the base of my bra.

Though my shorts are barely even a consideration, being flimsy and quite short, he peels them from my body anyway, taking my panties along with them.

In all the time we've known each other, and all the time we've been in compromising positions together, never once have I been so incredibly exposed to him. I'd be self-conscious if there wasn't hunger burning in his eyes.

He moves down my body, lowering himself between my legs and wrapping his strong arms tightly around my thighs. Before I even have a second to panic about what he's about to do, his tongue glides up my pussy and swirls around my clit. My gasp turns into a moan, back arching.

A hum pulls from his body, and he dives in deeper. My fingers fist into his hair, pulling him closer while digging my heels into the cushion to push away. It's the most polarizing feeling of needing more of his mouth, his tongue, and wanting to scramble off the couch at how overwhelming this is.

Never in my twelve years of being sexually active have I had sex anywhere other than the bed. Maybe the occasional shower. And here I am, first round with Zach and letting him taste me right on the couch in the middle of the living room. The only saving grace is that it's nighttime and we have the lights off for optimum movie watching. Otherwise, I'd be thoroughly anxious that a neighbor might see us.

"Fuck, Zach." The whine pulls from my chest as my head tips back, all while tugging at his roots.

He groans against me and pushes his tongue inside me before swirling it around my clit again. I knew he'd be able to use that tongue for far more than just kissing.

His movements become hurried, and he uses more pressure on my clit. I start to buck against his face, chasing his mouth, needing more.

As though he knows it's about to happen, he tightens his grip on my thighs and pulls them open a touch more as I crumble beneath him, shuddering and yanking his hair while I come with a whimper.

He supports me as I go limp, collapsing down to the couch, utterly exhausted. But my rest is short lived as he grabs my wrist and pulls me to sitting, yanking my shirt from over my head and quickly doing away with my bra.

I'm completely exposed to him. Every square inch of me is bare, and it takes me a second of humiliation to realize my hair is a complete mess.

But he's looking at me like he's never seen anything so beautiful. His lower lip is between his teeth, and he's sitting back on his heels, hands on his thighs as his gaze tracks every square inch of me.

"God, Mazie. You're so amazingly sexy." My cheeks warm at the way he says that compliment, his soft but husky tone making me shiver with desire. Reaching behind his head, he pulls his shirt off and tosses it to the side, immediately putting his hands on my thighs and sliding them up.

Zach with no shirt is certainly an incredible sight. I've always admired from afar, tried to ignore the fire that ignited in my belly and told myself I was just appreciating a good body and could do that without actually having feelings.

Now I realize I was an idiot.

Leaning up on my elbows, I trail my fingertips over his well-defined stomach and chest. My eyes follow the track of my fingers and when they get back to the hem of his jeans, a large bulge catches my attention.

Without thinking, I act on instinct and wrap my hand around it, giving a firm squeeze. His head tips back with a loud groan.

"Take these off." I hook my fingers through his belt loops and tug on the pants.

He hops off me and quickly kicks off his jeans, looking at me with raised eyebrows as his thumbs dip under the elastic of his boxer briefs.

Biting my lip, I give a quick nod and watch with wide eyes as he slowly shimmies them down. His cock bobs in front of him, rock hard. He gives himself a few rough strokes as he looks at me sprawled on the couch.

My thighs clench as he continues to stare. I don't know what to make of his silence or his very intent gaze as it rakes up and down my body.

"What are you doing?" Finally, I have to speak up.

"I just…it's all kind of hitting me at once. How much I've wanted this, how *long* I've wanted this. I need a minute to just make sure this is really happening."

My heart skips at his confession.

Leaning up, I reach for his hand and pull him down toward me. "It is," I murmur against his lips before looping a hand behind his neck and falling flat to the couch, taking him down with me.

He lowers himself so his hips press against mine and his erection is planted between us. Holding himself on his forearms, he hovers over me so his full weight isn't resting on me. His fingers brush a stray hair from my face.

"Last chance. You sure you want this?"

I tip up and brush my lips against his. "I'm sure."

The smile that spans his face is one I've never witnessed before, and I've seen Zach at some of his highest highs.

With a slight adjustment, he raises his hips and aligns himself. He gives me one more glance, to which I respond with a smile, before he eases himself into me.

My hands immediately fly to his shoulders, gripping hard as my head tips back with a low moan.

While it's been a long time since I've had sex, this is the most amazing it's ever felt right off the bat.

He keeps sliding in until he's all the way inside me, and he releases a shaky breath as he presses a kiss against my neck.

Slowly, he pulls out and then glides back in. He does it over and over, slow and steady, getting a feel for me and letting me get a feel for him. Then he starts to pick up speed.

And within a few moments, I feel when he stops holding back. It's like something in him snaps and he can't keep the beast inside any longer.

He takes my left leg and hooks it around his arm, opening me even further as he adjusts and moves deeper. Keeping his momentum going, he takes a quick glance behind him, before sliding back and pulling me with him.

Not only does it provide a new angle, but he starts thrusting harder and faster. He leans forward and pulls my nipple between his teeth.

"Holy shit! Zach."

"You have no idea how long I've waited to hear you say my name like that."

Yet some part of me does, because it's the same as the small part of me that's been wanting this to happen for years. The part of me that I buried deep down when everything turned upside down and Zach was the closest friend I had.

In the two weeks Zach was incommunicado, I had time to really think about our relationship. And I realized that there have always been instances when something would spark within me, some light would ignite before I quickly extinguished it. I couldn't risk losing Zach on what was surely a schoolgirl crush. I mean, the man is hot as hell. Who wouldn't have a crush on him?

Every time it made my heart ache when he had a girlfriend, and every relationship I tried that didn't feel right, I always chalked up to Zach just being my closest confidante. That I was scared I'd lose him as my best friend, and we wouldn't make time for each other anymore.

Only now, with him thrusting deep inside me and hovering over me, do I realize it has always been much more.

He slows and lowers so our chests are pressed together as he brushes his thumb down my face. "What's wrong? You're in your head. Should we stop? Was this a mistake?"

Though his eyes narrow and concern laces his features, I see hurt dancing through his irises.

Reaching up, I lock my hands behind his head, my thumbs resting in front of his ears. "Absolutely not. I'm just realizing how right this feels."

The smile that brightens his whole face is enough to make my heart burst.

Chapter 10
Zach

For a minute, I was sure she was going to tell me this was all a mistake. And, of course, it would be while I'm buried deep inside her and finally seeing the world clearly for what feels like the first time in my life.

But she didn't.

I crash my mouth to hers and tip my hips forward. She whines against my mouth, and I want to devour every sound she makes.

Mazie can get in her head, I know this. But I really felt like if she put too much thought into what was happening, she'd realize it's a mistake. That she'd shun me, and we'd never be the same again.

Instead, it seems like things are going my way. I definitely didn't expect this when I showed up tonight. We hadn't spoken since that first kiss, and I was missing her. Though I wasn't sure it would work, I hoped showing up for movie night would be enough to get back in her good graces, to pave over the hole I'd made in the road.

Thankfully, it's been beyond what I could have imagined.

I'm not a ladies' man. It's something that I pride myself on. I don't do one-night stands, I don't sleep around. Monogamy is the only option for me.

And even though it's been a while, I never dreamed sex could be this incredible.

It's taking everything I have not to come too fast. Now that she's distracted herself and thrown a slight wrench into things, I can't let us lose momentum.

Adjusting myself, I pull out and give a quick bite to her neck, grabbing her hips and flipping her to her stomach while pulling her knees down to the floor.

She's pushing up on her hands, which I grab and pull behind her back, holding them against her supple skin, just as above her ass, like I would with somebody I'm arresting. Then I push between her shoulder blades so her chest is flush against the couch.

A small smile plays on her face, but I know Mazie, and she's not adventurous. In fact, this whole thing is probably quite different for her.

With one hand, I keep her wrists bound behind her back and reach around to grab her breast. I swirl my fingers around her nipple, and she moans into the couch, pushing her ass out. Exactly the reaction I was hoping for.

I slip the tip of my cock through her soaking pussy and dive into her. She squeals at the sudden and full intrusion, clenching her muscles around my cock. My head tips back with a groan.

Though I've been trying to hold myself together, I feel the thread of self-restraint fraying. I prefer things a bit...rougher. I'm dying to smack her ass until it turns pink and warm. But I know that's not Mazie, and I'll hold myself back forever if that's what she wants.

So instead, I tighten my grip on her wrists and slowly pull out until just the tip of my cock is left inside her. Then, all at once, I slam my full length back in. Her upper body shifts forward on the couch.

I repeat the motion again, and again.

After a minute or two of repeating this, I pick up speed, thrusting into her with newfound vigor and force. Every single push in causes her to whine and moan, and each pull out has her tipping her ass higher in the air, like she's searching for my cock.

She may not be adventurous, but she is responsive.

"Zach."

Mmm. The way she says my name. So full of passion and desire. It unhinges me just a little more.

And causes me to start pumping into her in a way that may be considered too rough. But I keep a close eye on her face, carefully watching for any signs of pain or discomfort. Instead of either of those, her face crumples in ecstasy.

A tickling at my wrist makes me glance down to where I'm holding her hands firmly behind her back, to find her fingers wiggling against my arm. I adjust my grip, and she links her fingers with mine, squeezing tightly as her eyes shut and her mouth falls open.

She lets out a whimper and pulls her bottom lip between her teeth. "Fuck. I'm going to come."

Those words have never sounded so incredible.

I lean forward, resting my lips against her ear. "You like the feel of my cock inside you. Don't you, Mazie?"

"Yes." The word is a breathless pant.

Staying bent over her, I move a hand between her and the couch, my middle finger finding her clit and rubbing in a circular motion while I pound into her. She's going to be sore after this.

"Zach." She cries out my name as she starts to tremble, and her pussy clamps down on my cock.

It's so tight I can barely move, and I choke out a groan as I spill inside her. It catches me a little off guard. Usually, I'm better at edging myself, but she's just so damn perfect, and her body is incredible.

Aside from her back rapidly rising and falling, Mazie's completely still. Dread pours over me. Is she okay? Was I too rough for our first time? Did I hurt her?

But then a smile crosses her face, and she heaves a content sigh.

Glancing around for something to clean her up with, I settle on my undershirt. I grab it as I pull out of her, wiping up our mess before tossing the shirt to the side.

I flop to my back against the gray carpet, taking a breath. Mazie stays bent over the couch, and I reach out and smack her ass. She gives a tiny yelp, but the sound that resonates in my ears is that of my palm against her flesh.

She finally lies down next to me, her head on my chest and arm flung over me. One leg drapes over mine, and I can feel her wetness against my thigh. It makes my dick jump.

Though most of her body is cool to the touch, her breasts are warm. I put my hands on her shoulders and push her back, a wide smile pulling up the corners of my lips at seeing that her chest is raw and red. Seems like a touch of rugburn from the couch.

We're lying silently, and I'm staring up at the ceiling while I trail a finger along her arm, when she starts giggling. My eyebrows draw together and my hand halts.

"What's so funny?"

"I don't know. Isn't it all just a little...weird? Not in a bad way. It was *amazing*. But we've been best friends for years and know a *lot* about each other. But I never knew you were into anything rough."

"Is that...is it a problem? I know I probably should have checked with you or something, but this wasn't exactly planned."

"No. You're fine. It was...different than what I'm used to or have experienced before. But, I don't know, maybe that's better. Something unique between us."

"Can I make a confession?"

When her breathing halts, and she doesn't answer for a moment, worry creeps through my mind.

"Sure." But her word brings comfort back.

"I was not actually as rough as I like to be."

"Oh."

"The rawness of your chest right now? It's such a fucking turn on. I wanted to slap your ass red but wasn't sure how you'd feel about that. I didn't necessarily mean for it to be anything other than sensual, but you just do something to me that made me snap, and I couldn't hold back. I'm sorry."

She's already shaking her head before I'm done talking. "There's nothing to apologize for, Zach. I'm a grown woman, and I have a voice that I'm not afraid to use. Like I said, it was different. But the whole thing was. You're somebody I know so well, am so close to, and recognize in so many different ways that it wasn't as if we needed to learn about each other. It's like we just jumped right into the deep end and skipped swimming lessons."

"I'm still not sure if you think that's a good thing or bad thing."

She puts a palm against my jaw and leans up as she turns my face toward hers. Her lips brush gently against mine before she says, "It's a very good thing."

Though she moves to lie against me again, I lose my hand in the curls at the back of her head and pull her mouth to mine. My tongue sweeps between her lips and tangles with hers. This could get dangerous. I can't get enough.

But instead, I pull back and cup her cheek. "How are you feeling? You know what? Never mind."

I roll out from underneath her and scoop her up into my arms. She loops her hands around my neck but looks around frantically. "What are you doing?"

"I'm going to draw you a bath. You're likely to be sore after sex like that."

"Zach, I'm fine. Let's just go to bed."

"No."

She leans back and raises an eyebrow. I tighten my grip around her and start toward the bathroom.

"What do you mean 'no'?"

"If we're really doing this, which it seems like we are since I just fucked you relentlessly and I'm carrying you through your house naked, I'm going to take care of you. Always. It's not just to protect you from outside forces, but to care for you when you're sick, or hurt, or just need a fucking break. Mazie, you've been everything for your sisters for so long, it's time somebody be that for you."

Her mouth parts, as though she's about to protest, but it closes just as quickly. She leans her head against my shoulder and presses her lips to my neck. "Thank you."

Once we get into the bathroom, I start the faucet and put the plug in. One thing Mazie loves about this house is the old-fashioned claw foot bathtub.

Knowing Mazie as well as I do, and having been here as frequently as I have, I know where everything is. So as soon as I set her down, I can go about finding the jar of bath salts she uses and dump in roughly a cup's worth.

I set a towel on the floor, just outside the bath, where our feet will land so as not to make a puddle, because she hates having to clean things like that up. Then I grab two new towels from the closet.

It's not until I extend a hand to help her in that I take a glance at her. She's stunningly, achingly beautiful. But her arms are crossed against her chest and a light smile plays on her face.

"What's that pretty smile for?"

"You just...you fit here. You move so effortlessly, it's like you've lived here for years."

"In some ways, I have." I close the gap between us, putting a hand at her lower back and pulling her flush against me while the other cups her cheek, my thumb running along her cheekbone. "I know you, Mazie."

"Yeah. You do."

Though I could get lost in her sapphire eyes forever, I have to tear away. The longer we wait, the sorer she'll be.

I climb into the tub first, holding her hand while she daintily tests the water with her toes before moving all the way in.

The best thing about the clawfoot tub is that it's huge. There's plenty of room for both of us, and it has a nice, inclined back for me to lean against. Before I've even fully settled, I pull Mazie back against my chest, one arm around her shoulders.

Her head rests against my collarbone, and her curls tickle my chin. My body vibrates as she hums.

"What?"

One shoulder lifts slightly, and her hands glide through the water. "This just feels right. You know?"

"I'm glad you think so." Relief floods my body and seeps out with my words.

She turns slightly and tips her head back to meet my eye. "Were you worried?"

"Of course I was. Not only did I feel like you didn't want me to have kissed you, once it clicked you did...I don't know. What if we had sex and you felt like you made a mistake?"

"You could have felt the same way."

Before she finishes, I'm shaking my head. "Never. No single second has ever been a mistake with you, Mazie. Do I wish we got together sooner? Maybe. But our relationship has grown and blossomed and turned into something that brought us to where we are."

"Where exactly are we?" There's a hesitation to her tone, a true curiosity.

Is she serious? After that, how does she not know?

But wait. This is Mazie. The girl who overthinks like it's her job and questions her self-worth on a regular basis.

"I want you to be mine, Mazie. Exclusively. And all that entails. Dates, sleepovers, making dinner for each other. I want to be with you as often as possible. And, of course, more sex."

"Is it all going to be that rough?" Though her tone holds true curiosity, I can tell she's slightly concerned as well.

"Was it too much for you?" It's better I know now.

"It was just different. Not necessarily in a bad way."

"Mazie. I need you to be honest with me. I won't ever hurt you, and I won't do anything you don't want to do, but my proclivities tend to lean more to the rough side." Now's the moment she has to be honest. Will it change things? Truthfully, I'm not sure.

It's like there's a beast caged inside me that just needs to be let out sometimes, and if I can't do that with her, maybe there's just no hope for us after all. I hate to even think that way. Mazie's all I've wanted for longer than I even realize. But I'm not sure I can turn that part of me off.

When she doesn't answer, I take her chin in my hand and tip her face toward mine. "Answer me."

She tries to shrug away, but I won't let her. "Honestly, I don't know. I obviously enjoyed myself, and I know you did too. But that was my first time ever having sex outside of the bedroom."

My brows shoot sky high before my jaw clenches. There's shock mixed with anger and jealousy. Not that I have any right to feel that way, I could have told her a long time ago that I wanted to try things. Well, I guess I could have maybe figured it out for myself and told her. Though the more I think about it, the more I'm sure I was just lying to myself for years.

"Would it make you feel better if I told you I plan to fuck you in a bed plenty?" Though I'm trying to make light of things, she doesn't laugh.

I hang my forehead against her shoulder and take a deep breath. "How about a mix? I can rein myself in for you here and there if you're willing to be adventurous for me."

She nods slightly and licks her lips. "I can agree to that."

The water has started to chill. "Are you sore? Should I add more hot water?"

"No. I'm good. I'm tired, actually."

Trailing my lips along her supple skin from her shoulder to her neck, my dick pulsates, and I know I won't last long without being inside her again. "Can I stay the night?"

"I was hoping you would."

"With you. In your bed."

"Where else would you stay?" She sounds so confused. Like I haven't spent many a night in her guestroom. But before I can ask, she shakes her head and wipes her wet palm down my cheek. "You said we're doing this. Right? So if you're really going to make me yours, if you're going to protect me from everything, you need to be in bed next to me."

"Thank fuck." I crash my lips to hers, gripping her messy curls tightly as I tip her head back. As much as I want to stay in this tub and kiss her and fuck her, it's cold and it's time to stop when her body shivers, and not in the sexy way.

I separate myself from her and step out of the tub, chills racing down my spine as I wrap a gray towel around my waist. Grabbing a pink one from the hook, I hold it wide open for Mazie to step into. The second she does, I wrap it around her and rub my hands up and down her arms while I pull her against me. Briefly, I press my lips to the top of her head.

Part of me is tempted to scoop her up and carry her off to her bedroom, but a more rational part of me decides to let her lead the way.

She links her fingers through mine and pulls me into her room. Holding the towel tightly around her chest, she looks around the room before turning to face me. But she won't look me in the eye. "Um, I don't know what you want to wear."

"I'll just wear my boxers from before. That's usually all I wear to bed."

"Okay."

I run my fingers down her arm as I walk past her and into the living room. Our clothes are scattered all over the floor, and I scoop up every garment I can find.

Dropping them on the bed, I sift through them until I find my boxer briefs and tug them on. Mazie comes to stand next to me, still clad in her towel, and carefully picks through the clothes, her fingers delicately holding up my shirt.

Silently, she turns to look at me with raised eyebrows.

There are few things sexier than a woman wearing your shirt. I smile and nod.

I stifle a groan as she drops the towel and pulls the shirt over her head. Of course it's swimming on her and hangs below her ass. But she smiles and moves the rest of the clothes off the bed before turning down the covers.

At home, I normally sleep sprawled across the whole bed. But here, I'll have to be on one side. She crawls onto the bed and right up the middle, before settling down in the fetal position more on the right side of the bed.

I scoot in behind her and loop an arm around her waist, tugging her against me before pulling the blanket up to cover us both.

For the first time ever, I fall asleep wrapped around my best friend.

Chapter 11

Mazie

The brightness of the early morning sun pulls me from sleep. I blink a few times at the intrusion of light, utterly confused.

Then it hits me. I didn't close the curtains last night. Not in the bedroom, not in the living room. Did I lock the front door? What about the garage door?

My heart races, and my breathing rate picks up as I realize I failed to check all of my safety standards before going to bed.

The heavy arm flung over my waist tightens, and I'm pulled against a hard, warm chest. "Hey. You're okay."

For a moment, I completely forgot Zach was even here. That the events of last night even happened.

While a sense of safety washes over me, anger boils in my stomach. I know better than to ignore my routine. But Zach got me in such a tizzy that I lost my thought process. I can't let that happen again.

I roll to face him and am greeted with slits instead of open eyes. "How'd you know I was freaking out?"

"I know you, Mazie. I could practically feel your mind overthinking. What's wrong?"

"I didn't lock up like I usually do."

"You're safe with me. I won't let anything hurt you."

"It's not that simple."

He sighs heavily and runs a hand down my curls. "I know. But try to find solace in the fact that nothing happened. And besides, who would you call in the case of an emergency?"

"The cops," I mumble, knowing exactly where he's going with this.

"Well, wouldn't you know, I'm already here."

"But you're not armed. You're barely even dressed." I realize how ridiculous I sound. Juniper Grove is a relatively safe place. Zach handles Mrs. Henderson more than he does actual problems. But I know all too well that it only takes one bad person. It's how I lost my parents. It's how I almost lost my sister.

"Do you trust me?"

"Of course I do. But—"

"No. Mazie, I'm not going to convince you to stop doing your routine, especially if it makes you comfortable. But let last night go. You can't change it. I don't want you harping on it and worrying about it all day."

I take a deep breath and rest my hand against his chest. His steady heartbeat calms my erratic one. My eyes flutter closed, and I give myself a minute to relax. The reality of the situation is he's right.

Once I feel centered again, I open my eyes to meet his gaze. "Do you have to work today?"

"Off all weekend."

"How'd you get so lucky?" While Zach has Fridays off somewhat regularly, he usually ends up working Saturday or Sunday, if not both.

"Bianca managed to convince Steve to go on a vacation. For an entire week."

My eyebrows shoot to my hairline. Steve is one of the other cops on the force with Zach, and he is notorious for not missing a single day of work. He and his wife, Bianca, went to the courthouse on one of his days off to be married. No big wedding or anything. And they never took a honeymoon.

It's nice that she understands how seriously he takes his job, even if it does seem a little over the top at times. While Juniper Grove is a small town and not much happens here, the tragedy that struck my family has become a legend and something they talk about in the police unit.

Though it was a random occurrence, a harsh act of violence that came out of nowhere and hasn't been seen by this town since, it's still something to watch for. Especially when tourist season picks up. But just because I'm overly neurotic about my own safety, doesn't mean everybody else has to be.

"Wow. I'm honestly shocked. Good for her, though." An awkward silence envelops us. It's not so much that I'm uncomfortable with Zach being here, in my bed and practically naked. It's more so that this situation is so different from any I've found myself in with him before. Because, well, he's practically naked.

Not to mention, everything that transpired last night. Despite the bath, I'm sore in places I haven't been since my first time, maybe ever. It's both a good and bad feeling. Nobody likes to be uncomfortable or hurting, but the memory of what transpired between us makes me tingle all over.

Tipping my chin up with his thumb, he brushes his lips across mine before tucking a curl behind my ear. I don't even want to think about what a rat's nest my hair must be. It was a mess last night, and that was before the sex and sleeping.

"Let me make you breakfast." His voice is thick with sleep.

"I can cook, and you can rest more."

His arm tightens around my middle as he pulls me closer. "No, no. I want to cook for you."

Though I don't want to ask, I am curious if Zach can even cook. While he's my best friend, it's never really come up before. He either comes here for dinner, spends the night and I cook breakfast, or we get takeout. He's never cooked for me, and as far as I know, all he can do is grill hot dogs and burgers.

"Okay." I hope it doesn't come out as hesitantly as I feel.

A wide smile spans his face, and he hops out of bed, padding out into the kitchen in only his boxer briefs.

My brows furrow as I scramble out of bed, sliding into my house slippers and following him to the kitchen.

"You're not going to get dressed?" I tug at the hem of my shirt as I ask. While it's his and huge on me, it still doesn't cover much more than my ass and an inch of thigh.

He lifts a single shoulder as he pulls out a frying pan. "Wasn't planning on it."

"So, what are you making?"

"My specialty."

"And what is that?"

He glances over his shoulder at me as though I've offended him.

"What? You've never once cooked for me before. Not even a sandwich."

His gaze darts up to the ceiling and his face scrunches as though he's replaying a movie in his head. "Huh. I guess you're right." With another quick shrug, he turns around and grabs the eggs from the fridge.

I settle into a seat at the table to watch him. All the muscles in his body aid him in his cooking, rippling in exactly the right ways as he cracks and scrambles the eggs. While I was initially concerned about his lack of clothing because of the neighbors, I'm now extremely appreciative he opted to skip the shirt.

Watching Zach move through my kitchen so seamlessly is both unnerving and somehow comforting at the same time. He definitely seems at home here, but nobody else has ever cooked in my kitchen before. Not even Alina, aside from maybe heating up a premade meal.

Within just a few minutes, he's setting down two plates and cups of coffee. The only thing on the plates are eggs. No potatoes, no toast, not even bacon. Hm.

He sits next to me with a wide smile on his face, clearly very proud of himself.

Hesitantly, I take my fork and prod at the eggs. They seem both undercooked and overcooked at the same time.

I take a small bite and choke it down, turning to Zach with a smile on my face.

But his drops. "You don't like them."

"What? No. I—"

"M. Don't lie. I know you too well to know when you're not telling the truth."

"Fine. They're not very good. Is this *just* eggs?" I raise one eyebrow and point my fork at them in the process.

His face crumples in confusion. "Um. Yeah? Is it not supposed to be?"

Fighting a laugh, I rest my hand on his thigh. "Eggs by themselves don't taste great. You typically want to add something like milk or cheese or seasoning."

His cheeks flush pink. "Oh. I didn't know that. I've always done just eggs. We don't all have a chef sister to teach us these things, you know." There's a touch of irritation in his voice, and I know he's trying not to point out the glaringly obvious, which is that my mother taught us the basics, and his was barely around.

"Can you cook anything else? What do you have for dinner most nights?"

"I eat a lot of pasta." The words come out somewhat ashamedly. "Or do takeout. Or eat with you."

I turn in my chair to face him, and he does the same, putting his legs on the outside of mine. My arms loop around his neck, and I press my lips to his. "Hey. It's okay. I don't mind cooking for us. And maybe we can teach you a thing or two in the process."

"Or you can do the inside cooking, and I'll handle all the grilling."

"That works too."

"Well, if we're not going to eat this, what are we going to eat?" He pushes the plate away.

"What are you in the mood for?"

"Eggs."

I hang my head and giggle. "Okay. I'll throw together some new eggs. With some additions, if that's okay?"

"Absolutely."

With another quick kiss, I collect our plates, empty them into the trash, and get to making new scrambled eggs, with a dash of milk and some shredded cheddar cheese this time.

Grabbing a second pan, I get it warm and lay some bacon in it before popping four pieces of bread into the toaster.

I'm about to mix the eggs when strong arms loop around my waist. Zach's nose runs up the side of my neck and along my jawline before he nips at my earlobe.

"Have I told you yet that you look incredibly sexy in my shirt?" His fingertips glide along my thigh and slide up under the hem of my shirt, trailing along my stomach until he closes his hand around my breast.

My head tips back against his collarbone.

"How do you feel this morning?"

I don't have to ask him to elaborate. "A little sore."

Without another word, he pulls his hand from my shirt and backs away.

I spin around so quickly I nearly drop the spatula. "Where are you going?"

"I have to stay away from you before I can't control myself anymore. The floodgates are open now, M."

Taking a step closer, I run my free hand down his chest and lean my pelvis into his. "Then why are you stopping?" Though I try to use my sultry voice, I'm not sure it reads. I'm way out of practice and never thought I'd talk in such a way to Zach. I'm sure I sound ridiculous.

His fingers wrap around my wrist and pull my hand from his body while his other hand closes around my waist and he takes a step closer, effectively pushing me backward a touch. He's standing so close that every breath has my breasts brushing his chest and my head is craned back so I can look into his eyes.

Lust and primal need dance through his irises and never before have I felt so small in comparison to him.

"Because I'm not going to hurt you."

"What happened to taking some things slow and steady?"

"I'm a big man, Mazie. I'm not sure your spindly little legs can handle me being between them."

My brows crunch together, and I move from his embrace. "So, then what is this? Hey, thanks for a solid fuck last night. How about some breakfast, and I'll go?"

"Did I say that?"

"Well, if you're not willing to have sex with me, then..."

"I didn't say that either. I don't want to hurt you. So right now is not the time. Besides, I'm starving. I wouldn't be able to perform at my best, and that's what you deserve."

When I continue to stare blankly at him, a smirk pulls up one corner of his mouth, and he leans in so his lips brush my ear. "There are many other things that don't involve penetration, M."

A chill rushes down my spine as I think about him using that incredible tongue of his again.

"Let's have breakfast, and then I'll eat my midmorning snack." He nips at my earlobe before pulling away.

For a moment, I'm stunned still, but then a crackle from the pan behind me has me turning around to check the food.

My shoulders slump and corners of my mouth tick down as I note that half the bacon is, at the very least, extra crispy. I pull all the pieces out and lay them on a paper towel to soak up some of the grease. The bottoms of the eggs are slightly overdone as well, but not beyond repair.

I flip off the burner and get everything situated on the plates, trying to ignore the burning heat on my neck that's radiating from Zach's stare. The toast must have popped during our exchange, and the butter is barely melting.

"Sorry for the mediocre breakfast," I grumble as I set the plates down.

He leans over and kisses my temple. "Not a problem. Besides, I like crispy bacon." A smile spans his face as he pops a piece in his mouth and crunches it loudly.

Without a second thought, he digs in, a small 'mmm' escaping. But I'm not as eagerly devouring my breakfast, mostly pushing it around on my plate. My eyes keep dashing to the side, glancing at Zach as he consumes his breakfast.

"You're right. These are way better with some things added." His fork points to his plate, and he talks around a mouth full of eggs. But when he looks over at me, he swallows harshly, and his gaze darts from my plate back to my face a few times. "You're not eating."

"I am. A little."

Taking my chin in his fingers, he turns my face to his. "What's wrong?"

"This isn't weird to you?"

His face loses all of its color and his shoulders droop. "Uh, no. Is it bothering you?"

My heart races as I realize he misunderstood my meaning. I rest my wrists on his shoulders and run my fingertips through his hair. "It's not weird in a bad way, Zach. It's just...different. I mean, we've had breakfast together before. But you're not usually almost naked and not after a night of...what we did." My cheeks burn at the memory.

While I choose not to know too much about Alina and Liv's sex lives, they've always made fun of me for not being able to "girl talk" without blushing. And talking to Zach about it has never once happened. Though he's the one I was with, it still leaves an uncomfortableness settled in my bones. It's not how I want to feel, especially not about this. But I can't seem to get the feeling to go away.

"Do you want me to leave?" He raises an eyebrow and hikes his thumb over his shoulder.

"No. I definitely don't. My mind just needs a little time to wrap around this. What it is, what it entails. We've been so close for so long, and it's just, it's a whirlwind."

"How can I help?" The thing about Zach is that he knows me so well. He seems to understand how my mind functions, better than my siblings sometimes.

"Just be patient with me. I *want* this, I *want* to be with you. It's just taking my brain a little longer to make the switch from friends to friends with benefits?" I ask the last part hesitantly. We haven't exactly discussed what we are aside from the fact that we're now sleeping together.

"Try again." His head tips to the side, and his eyes narrow.

"Um…" I don't want to put words in his mouth. I don't want to make any assumptions for what we're doing here.

"Boyfriend and girlfriend." He says it so surely, like it's the only possible option.

"Are you sure?"

"Where's the doubt suddenly coming from, Mazie? I thought we were on the right track, that you wanted this." Though he's trying to mask it, I can hear the hurt seeping through his words, his shoulders tensing to recoil from me.

I cover my face with my hands and shake my head. "I'm afraid I'm not expressing myself clearly."

"I'm afraid that you are." He straightens and pulls out of my space, my hands falling to my lap.

Shit. I'm fucking this all up. I'm getting in my head too much about it, and I don't even know how or why. "I feel like I don't know how to act around you now."

"Why? Nothing's different."

"*Everything* is different."

"Mazie, the only thing that's changed is that we're sleeping together. Literally and figuratively. I don't understand why you're getting so in your head about this."

"Because what if you realize you don't like me anymore once we've been dating for a while? Then I lose my boyfriend *and* my best friend."

"I know you better than most people. Why would I suddenly stop liking you? The only difference between before and now is that we'll be having sex and spending nights together in the same bed instead of separate rooms."

"What if you don't like who I am? Maybe you only spend just enough time with me to not be turned away." My chin drops to my chest as my eyes burn.

With a firm finger under my chin, Zach raises my face until our eyes meet. "Hey. I like you for you. I know you, Mazie. On a deep and personal level. I've been through what are arguably the worst times of your life with you. And also some of the best. Is it possible that we'll find out we don't work as a couple? Sure. But that doesn't mean our friendship has to burn down in flames because of it."

"You think you'd still be able to be my friend if our relationship failed?"

"It'd be hard initially, but we were friends first. I don't see why it'd be impossible to go back to that. Maybe a little weird or awkward at the beginning, considering we now know what the other person looks like naked, but not out of the realm of possibility."

It's as though that was the last string holding me back. The last thing that was weighing heavily on my mind. Suddenly, I feel light and free. A smile takes over my face, and I bite my lower lip.

Because he's right. He *does* know me. Exceptionally well. And despite all of that, despite my pitfalls and neuroses and self-sabotaging ways, he still wants to be with me.

Chapter 12
Zach

Mazie's hesitation is throwing me for a loop. She seemed sure. I tried to make sure she was ready before anything happened last night. I don't want her to have any regrets, and now I'm wondering if that's exactly how she feels.

Is this weekend going to end and is she going to let me go on my merry way before letting me know that's it?

Where's the confidence she seemed to have last night? She was so set in the fact that she wanted this, wanted us, yet this morning she seems...afraid.

But now I'm left not knowing what to do, how to act. Does she even want me here? While I know Mazie so well, I'm having trouble truly reading her and what her wishes are right now. She says she wants me here, and after insisting on cleaning up from breakfast, she took my hand and led me over to the couch, where we're now snuggled up and watching a documentary about Earth. She loves these damn things.

Yet something still feels off. There's an awkwardness that I can't quite describe or pinpoint. Her legs are thrown over my lap while my finger idly trails up and down her thigh and her head rests against my shoulder. Everything should feel right. But it doesn't.

It makes an ache settle in my chest because last night it felt like things were finally clicking into place. Like everything I have wanted for years was finally becoming a reality. And now I'm not so sure.

Though I try to contain it, a sigh escapes me as I lower in my spot.

Her shoulders go back in the slightest adjustment that most others wouldn't notice.

Fuck this. "I should probably go, M. You don't seem to want me here."

Before I can even move and shift her legs off of me, she adjusts so she's straddling me, her arms tight around my neck. "Don't go. Please."

I hesitate for a minute, my hands out in front of me before wrapping them around her waist. "Help me out here, M. I don't know what to do."

"That's the problem. I don't know either. It's like I don't know how to act now."

"I don't understand why anything has to be different."

"Because I feel like I have to be somebody different. Girlfriend worthy. Like you'll expect more from me now or something. That boring, old, everyday Mazie isn't enough for you." Her voice trails off at the end and her forehead drops to my shoulder.

Gliding my hands up her back, I swoop them over her shoulders so I can take her face between my palms. I pull her back so that I can look into her gorgeous sapphire eyes. They're filled with pain that I know is stemming from her self-doubt. Mazie's had it rough, and she's never been one who believes in herself. And she surely doesn't realize how stunning she is, even right now in one of my old t-shirts and her auburn curls all over the place.

"I don't want you to be anybody other than who you are, Mazie. *That's* the girl I want. You."

"But—"

I'm shaking my head before she gets any further. "There are no buts, M. I know you see yourself as complicated, that others have said you're difficult. But you're neither of those things to me. Yes, you're...complex, but not in a bad way and not in any way I don't feel I can handle."

"What about this morning?"

My brows furrow, and I tip my head to the side, utterly confused as to what she's talking about.

"The doors." Her face pinkens. She's embarrassed by her need to check things and have them be a certain way.

"It's not about you being complex. It's not about changing your routine. It's that I want you to realize and trust that you're *safe* with me. I won't let anything happen to you. I've always been just a call away, and when I'm here, I just want you to understand that it's okay to make mistakes. I won't ask you to stop checking the locks and doors, in fact I'll probably take over that responsibility the nights I'm here. But I don't want you to fixate on it in case we forget or fall asleep on the couch and amble to bed at two in the morning."

"It doesn't bother you? That I check the locks three times, or have to leave for places a little early so I can double or triple or quadruple check that the door's really locked?"

"No, Mazie. Because I understand it. You've been through so much, and that instilled a fear in you that makes perfect sense. Not to mention, you jumped right from sister in mourning to trying to be the best mother figure you could. And that took on a lot of concern for your sisters. I'm pretty sure you've spent the last twelve years living in nothing but a state of fear."

She sits back slightly, her ass on my thighs, and I trail my hands down her back to rest around her waist. Her eyes dart between mine, and I'm wondering what she's thinking, still not being able to read her, when she leaps forward and crashes her mouth to mine.

I'm stunned still for a moment, not at all having expected this. But then my mouth moves against hers, my tongue slipping between her lips as I try to lose my hand in her hair. It's all piled up and pulled back and I can't get a good grip.

With a slight movement, I stop the kiss and work to undo her hair.

Her hands fly up to cover mine and stop me. "What are you doing?"

"Taking your hair down."

"It's a mess."

"I don't care."

The corners of her lips pull up in a slight smile, and she undoes her hair, letting it fall around her shoulders. Though it's a bit frizzy with curls sticking out at odd angles and much of the top has lost its curl pattern, she's stunning. I run my hands over the top of her head and down her hair until they settle on her lower back. "You're gorgeous."

I lose a hand in the mess of her hair like I had been trying to do before, pulling her mouth back to mine as I lift my hips to press against her. I'm already hard and straining against my boxer briefs.

With a tug, her head tips back, and I lick from the base of her neck to her ear, pulling her earlobe between my teeth.

Her fingers fly to my chest and flutter against my skin.

"You ready to take me again?" The words rumble out of me, against her cheek.

She digs her nails into my chest and nods silently.

Gentle. I have to remember to be gentle. Not only because she told me she's sore, but because I promised her I wouldn't be rough every time. I need to show her that I'm listening, that I heard her.

Making sure I have a solid hold on her, I rise from the couch, and she loops her legs around my waist and her arms around my neck. She's clinging to me like a baby monkey.

While I happily know next to nothing about Mazie's sex life, I can say without a shadow of a doubt that nobody has ever treated her the way I will. Like the Goddamn princess she is.

When we get to her bedroom, I sit her on the edge of the bed, quickly reaching down to pull my shirt from her body. I toss it over my shoulder and rest my hands on either side of her, leaning in until she falls back against the mattress with a giggle.

Bending at the waist, I kiss along her lower belly, from hipbone to hipbone before lowering. Pushing her panties to the side, I lick straight up her pussy. Her back arches off the bed with a moan.

I dive in for more, wrapping my arms around her thighs and pulling her closer as I kneel on the ground before her. I devour her like she's my last meal, slipping my tongue up and down her pussy, around her clit, and pushing it inside her. She's writhing and moaning beneath me, and I can't believe I waited so long to make her mine, to hear the incredible sounds she makes when my face is between her thighs. The good news is that Mazie tastes even better than I could have imagined.

She's like the sweetest, most delectable drug, and I've already become an addict.

Her fingers dive into my hair, yanking at the roots as her body starts to tremble. That's when I close my lips around her clit, sucking hard and flicking my tongue against it. Her legs wrap around my head and her body practically levitates off the bed as she screams and trembles, filling my mouth with deliciousness.

Once she stops moving, her legs fall to the side and her fingers loosen in my hair. I kiss along the insides of her thighs, pulling her panties from her legs and tearing off my boxers.

I slide my body over hers, gliding my parted lips up her torso. Her breathing is hard and erratic. I lay lingering kisses along her collarbone and jaw while hovering over her.

"I'm sorry." Her eyes remain closed.

My brows pull together, and I wipe a stray curl from her forehead. "For what?"

"For...what I just did."

"You mean for very sexily coming on my tongue?" I bend to flick my tongue against her nipple. "Is that what you mean?"

"Yes." It comes out breathily as I continue to swirl my tongue on her breast.

"Mmm. Don't ever apologize for that."

Her eyes pop open and she tries to lean up on her elbows. "You mean...you mean you liked it?"

"Of course. Why wouldn't I?"

Pink rushes to her cheeks. "It's just...I've done that before and the guy I was with at the time thought it was gross."

My jaw ticks in irritation, and not just because of the thought of Mazie with another man. "Well, that guy's a fucking idiot. It's sexy as hell. Especially knowing that *I* can make you feel that way."

The corner of her lower lip is pulled between her teeth. "How else can you make me feel?"

With a smirk, I pull her nipple into my mouth and flick the hardened peak with my tongue. She arches against me, and I slide my hand down her body to settle between her legs. A moan pulls from my chest as I feel how soaked she is.

With a quick graze of my teeth, I release her nipple and ease my cock into her. A tiny whimper bleeds through her lips as her hands latch to my shoulders.

Her breath hitches once I'm firmly inside her. She feels so fucking incredible.

Slowly, I pull out to the tip, and then lower my hips to glide back in. While I typically prefer hard and fast, there's something to be said about slow and steady with Mazie. I don't want it to be over as quickly, as there's not just the end goal I'm trying to reach. The intimacy that I've always felt was lacking in relationships is here. It's strong.

It's in the way Mazie's fingers grip my skin, the way her eyelids flutter as I thrust, the tiny moans she makes every time I plunge back into her. The way her breathing deepens the more I continue.

"Zach." And absolutely in the way she pants my name.

It does something to me, and I have to stop myself from getting out of control. From flipping her to her stomach and shoving her face into the mattress while I slam into her. Or hooking her ankles behind my head and railing her so hard the whole bed moves.

That's not what she wants right now, and I promised I'd be gentle. So instead, I swallow down the urges and close my hand around her hip, my fingertips digging in a little harder than they should. Some part of me feels proprietary over Mazie, that she's mine and I can brand her with my body.

The more I pump into her, the more pleasured sounds come from her parted mouth. While Mazie's voice has always had a calming musical quality to it, I never knew it could be so fucking sexy. Things between us haven't just shifted, they've completely altered course.

"Fucking hell, Mazie. You're so damn sexy. It makes me so hard." Sometimes painfully so. I give a few quick thrusts that cause her head to tip back and her nails to dig into my biceps.

"God, Zach. How do you know all the right things to say?"

I lick up her neck and nibble her earlobe. "Because I know you, M. Better than anybody else could, and now on every level." My hand latches onto her chestnut headboard, and I use it to drive myself deeper inside her while she moans and writhes beneath me.

Her breaths become shuddery and her fingers twitch against my skin. She makes the most amazing face when she comes; crumpled in ecstasy, her perfectly pink plump lips wide apart as she takes a deep breath. When her pussy clenches around my cock, she moans loudly, body trembling.

My hand slides from her hip to cup her ass, and I squeeze her flesh while driving my cock into her a few more times before I come deep inside her, my face pointing skyward. Being with Mazie is like nothing else. Even the orgasms feel more intense. And I've only had two so far.

Staying inside her, I keep my grip on the headboard and drop my forehead to hers. Her heavy breaths caress my face all I want to do is feel her mouth around my cock. Especially while I hold a handful of her hair.

"Still not sure how to act around me?"

"A little. We can't just have sex all the time."

"Are you sure about that?"

She swats at my shoulder while I chuckle and ease out of her, grabbing some tissues from the nightstand to clean her up with.

I flop to my side and rest my cheek on my elbow. "Just be you, Mazie. There's nothing else I want."

She mimics my pose, turning to face me. "Okay, I get that, but what are we supposed to do?"

"Anything you want. Don't change your routine or schedule just because I'm here. What do you usually do over the weekend?" Though we're best friends, we don't exactly know what the other does every waking hour of every day. I know she gets some work in seven days a week, even if from home and not the café. But what she does in her spare time isn't something I'm overly familiar with. Sure, I know her hobbies, but not how often she entertains those. I used to be a lot more familiar with her days before I became a cop and started working crazy hours.

"Usually a little work. I've been having Alina change the specialty sandwich every week, and she's trying to come up with a new pastry each week too. So on Saturday, I usually head over to Three Sticks to update the signs."

It's one of the homier touches of their café. Mazie has hand-written and doodled on all of the chalkboard signs that they have as menus. She's always had a bit of an artsy flare, and I was worried it'd be squashed when she went to college for her MBA. I'm happy she found a way to still keep her artistic side alive, at least a little.

"Okay. What else?"

"I usually do grocery shopping on Sunday for as much of the week as I can so I don't have to go back to the store. Otherwise, I mostly just hang out. I often take a nap because my anxiety meds make me sleepy. Read a little, maybe paint a bit. Clean." It's hard to believe there's anything left to clean, but I'm sure that's how it stays so spotless.

"Alright, well, you can do all of those things with me if you want. I don't mind helping you clean or tagging along to the café or grocery store. I'm perfectly fine entertaining myself around the house if you want to be alone while you read or paint." She doesn't look convinced, the corners of her mouth pointing down. "All I'm saying, M, is that you don't have to do anything differently. You don't have to work me into your routine. I'm here to be with you. That's it."

"You won't get bored?"

"I don't bore easily. Besides, I like watching you. And definitely don't mind zoning out to some TV." I wouldn't exactly say I have a stressful job, especially not in Juniper Grove. But it's nice to be able to take off the uniform and not have to be on alert for a few hours.

Her fingers pick at the sheet for a few minutes, and I know she's contemplating what to do. And then it suddenly hits me. Mazie's not uncomfortable that I'm here. It's that she doesn't want me to feel pressured to stay.

"What—" I run a hand through my hair and take a deep breath, not sure I really want to be asking this question but may as well. "What did you do with other boyfriends?" One of my eyebrows rises.

Her eyes widen and her cheeks flame. "Honestly, I never spent a ton of time at home with them. Maybe a quick date or brief night together, but never just spending a weekend together unless we went on vacation. Which happened once for a short weekend getaway. But they were mostly just guys I was dating, not something I'd necessarily consider a relationship."

Hm, the fact that she makes this distinction is interesting.

"Listen. I don't want to do anything that's going to make you uncomfortable, so if it's better for me to leave, just let me know. My feelings won't be hurt. Well, not too terribly. But if you want me to be here, that's plenty for me. Because I just want to be around you, Mazie." I reach out and brush a curl behind her ear before trailing my fingers along her jaw.

The smile that spans her face is enough to make me want to quit my job and never leave this bed again.

Chapter 13
Mazie

I don't know why I've been so in my head about Zach being here. It's really starting to mess with me. He's my comfort, yet I feel the need to be something *more* for him now that we're together.

Thankfully, he's taken everything in stride and isn't frustrated with me. I couldn't see beyond my boring day-to-day existence and what would be so interesting about that. But I realized it's not about being interesting to him, it's about spending time together. Which is definitely what I want.

While I've always dreamed of having a husband and children, at a certain point within the past few years, I've all but given up on that dream. It's hard to think you'll have something when you barely even make an effort to date. Hard to get married without a significant other.

But over the course of the past eighteen hours, and perhaps even the past two weeks, Zach's reignited that hope. If only just because he's showing me that I'm somebody worth dating, worth simply being with, because it's all he wants to do.

It feels natural to be together like this. Right. For some reason, I couldn't wrap my head around the fact that my sisters surely don't do every single thing with their husbands, and likely just coexist together much of the time they're both home. A lot of it falls to the fact that I've never been in a relationship where my boyfriend wanted to spend that much time together. I never really let the relationship progress that far, and with Zach, there was no buildup; we jumped right in.

Or maybe the buildup has been the past twenty years.

He's truly comfortable here, enjoying his time in my vicinity. Every now and again when I glance over at him lounging on the couch—which I can't help but do every few minutes—he'll give me a wide smile that makes my heart race.

And any time he gets up, he'll press a kiss against my temple before moving through the house to use the bathroom or pour more coffee.

Knowing he's not expecting me to entertain him has made my shoulders relax and the knot ease from my back.

When my stomach rumbles, I'm sure Zach's hungry too. With a stretch, I set down my paintbrush, not that the inspiration has been a good friend to me today. Aside from the rough outline of a daisy, the only painting I actually got in were a few strokes for blades of grass.

"Hey." I stand by the foot of the couch while Zach lies on his back, one arm under his head, the other resting over his chest while he holds the remote. There's a baseball game on the TV. "I was thinking of making some lunch. Hungry?"

His eyes dart to me, then back at the TV when he winces, shakes his head, grumbles, and hits the power button so the screen goes black. "The Yanks are killing me this year," he mostly mumbles to himself. "Yeah. Lunch would be great. Can I help?"

"Are your lunch-making skills as disastrous as your breakfast skills?" I pull my lips between my teeth so I don't smile too widely.

"Worse, actually. I usually just grab a granola bar."

I roll my eyes and shake my head. How, after all this time, did I not know this man was so hopeless in the kitchen? "Well, I was just thinking something like sandwiches. Quick and easy."

"Sounds perfect. You can teach me how to make a perfect one." He winks and his hand grips my hip.

One thing that's certainly changed is that now, every single time he touches me, electricity zings through my veins.

"Turkey okay with you?"

"Not picky, M. Don't overthink this."

"It's not overthinking to be considerate of your preferences." Is it?

"When have you ever known me to turn down food?" He has a point there. The man works out to stay fit for his job, and then some, but my God, does he pack it away.

Thanks to Alina, there are almost always high-quality rolls and breads to be had. While we sell them at the bakery for purchase, she likes to make sure we're all fully loaded. Eli usually has to make multiple trips to the car with how much she gives him to stock up on. And he freezes most of it, which Alina considers highly offensive to the bread.

When we first opened, he used to come in a lot more often. Now, it's become much less frequent for a random Eli visit. It'd hurt if I didn't understand that he needs the time away, the space. It's not that he doesn't love us, but he sacrificed so much that it weighs heavily on him. Especially when he sees the success of the café. He's happy for us, elated. But he was destined for so much more than being a college professor.

Mom and Dad wouldn't be disappointed. I don't think they ever could be disappointed in their golden boy. But it's certainly not what any of us expected from him.

Regardless, it makes sense why he changed trajectory. But since the girls are older, since we've opened the café and found success, I've encouraged him more than once to consider going back to MIT. That we'd be okay without him for the time he's away. He's always refused. Sometimes it's as hard for him to leave the protector role behind as it is for me to leave the mother role behind.

A throat clearing behind me pulls me from my thoughts, and I realize I've been standing in the pantry, holding a bag of kaiser rolls for what's likely longer than normal. I shake away lingering guilt, closing the pantry door, and setting the rolls on the counter.

Feeling a little embarrassed, I don't make eye contact with Zach while I gather the rest of the ingredients, spending a few extra seconds looking in the fridge while I take some deep inhales and exhales to calm my anxiousness.

Once I have everything in front of me, I smile at him and clap my hands once. "Okay. What would you like on your sandwich?"

He takes a step closer and loops an arm around my waist, tugging my side against his chest. "Anything you want to throw on there."

"I like my turkey sandwiches a little plain. Some mayo, lettuce, tomato. That's usually it. Sometimes I throw cucumbers on top too."

His lips press against the top of my head. "I told you, I'm not picky."

"I know. But I'm saying you *can* be. If there's something you want on your sandwich, let me know."

"Hmm. Got any peppers?"

"What kind?" I tend to keep myself well stocked in fruits and vegetables.

"I was thinking bell, but I'd take a spicy variety too." With a squeeze to my hip, he lets go so I can see what I have available.

Opening the vegetable crisper, I dig through to see what I have. Finally, under a bag of carrots and some spinach, I find a lone red bell pepper and hold it up in victory.

"Alright! You should put some on yours too. Adds a nice extra flavor."

"I might just give that a try." Pulling out a cutting board from the drawers to my right, I bump it closed with my hip and grab a knife. Carefully and diligently, I start slicing up the vegetables. Though Mom taught me a handful of things in the kitchen, I've learned most of what I know from my sister. While she may focus more on pastry and breads, her chopping skills are unparalleled.

Being so focused on the task at hand, I don't notice that Zach has stepped behind me until his chest presses against my back and fingers glide down my arms. His shuddery breath shifts a loose curl and sends a shiver racing down my spine.

"Be careful. I have a sharp knife in my hands." The words come out with little conviction.

His lips trail across my shoulder and up my neck, my head tipping back against his collarbone as I grip the handle of the knife tightly. "Unless you're going to turn around and stab me with that knife, I don't care about it." To further express his point, he unfurls my fingers and removes the handle, sliding it across the counter and out of reach.

When his hand grips my very messy bun, all I can think about is how badly I need to wash my hair. Until he pulls my head to the side and nibbles along my neck. The cucumber I was peeling drops to the cutting board with a thud, and Zach pushes it to the side.

Releasing my hair, his hand moves down my neck and presses between my shoulder blades so my chest flattens against the granite.

His rock-hard cock pushes against my ass, and I stifle a moan, all too needy for him to fill me again.

While keeping a palm against my back, his other hand glides under my shirt and across my lower stomach. His fingers dive into my panties, immediately finding my clit, and giving a few swirls before sliding easily inside me.

My legs part wider, and my breath catches.

"Keep your chest down, Mazie."

I nod my response as his fingers hook inside me. My nails try to find traction on the smooth surface of the counter, a whine pulling from my chest as he removes his touch. It's almost cruel leaving me on edge, but I'm sure he knows that.

His hands smooth up my thighs and over the swell of my ass, gliding my shirt up with them. Hooking his thumbs under the elastic of my panties, he pulls them down, gently lifting my legs one at a time to remove the garment. Anticipation swirls through me as he kisses up my legs, alternating sides on his way up.

My body lurches forward, and I hear the crack of his hand against my ass before I feel the sting. It's new and different, but I can't say it's terrible.

He lines himself up at my entrance, slipping through my wetness before plunging into me. We both share a moan, and his fingers grip tightly around my hips as he pushes me forward and back with each thrust.

My breasts drag along the counter and the icy sensation against my hardened nipples in comparison to the rising heat of my body creates an odd mingling. It's like I want to sweat and break into chills at the same time.

"Z-Zach."

There's another swift smack of my ass. I pitch forward again with a whine.

A low growl fills my ears as he continues to pound into me. Every few thrusts, there's another palm to my skin. There's a burning singing along my cheeks, but it hurts in a delicious way I would've never expected.

While I've had more sex in the past twenty-four hours than I've ever had in a single weekend, maybe Zach's opening me up to some new ideas in the bedroom.

"God, Mazie. Your ass looks so incredible hot and red." His words have me clenching tighter around his length.

"Oh, God."

He slams into me and grips my hair, pulling me up on my fingertips. "Try again."

"Z-Zach?"

"That's right. Don't ever forget who's making you feel this good. And it's definitely not God, baby." Who knew this man had such a dirty mouth?

And more so, who knew I'd like it?

Not just that, but the sting on my backside, the pinching at my scalp as Zach continues to hold my head back while pounding into me. While after the first time I told him I needed him to be gentle, I'm quickly changing my mind.

He's making me want more than just sex. He's making me want to be *fucked*. Which is something I've never craved before.

Releasing my hair, his hands enclose over both breasts, and he twists my nipples between his thumbs and forefingers.

My head falls forward, and my hands grip the edge of the counter as I start to shudder. He slows his thrusts as I ride out my orgasm but makes each slam a little harder, reaching a spot inside me that has me seeing stars.

A choked groan is the only sound from his lips as he tightens his grip on my breasts and holds himself deep inside me, finding his release.

His forehead drops to my upper back, and we both pant heavily for a few minutes before he lets go of me, reaching to the side to grab the hand towel off the oven handle.

With a quick cleanup, he tosses the towel to the side and grabs the back of my neck, spinning me around to face him.

"Are you okay?" Concern laces his features as his brows pull together.

"Why wouldn't I be?" I ask breathlessly.

"I let myself lose a little bit of control there. I'm sorry."

Pushing up on my toes, I press a quick peck to his lips. "Don't be."

His hand trails down my spine, and I spin away, reaching across the counter and pulling the cutting board back into my space and leaning the other way for the knife.

I can practically feel confusion swirling off of Zach, who's still standing behind me, as I go back to slicing up the vegetable for our sandwiches, feeling rejuvenated but even hungrier than I was before.

He leans his elbow against the counter. "Um. Care to explain?" He reaches out and grabs a piece of pepper, popping it into his mouth.

Without looking in his direction, I keep chopping. "We had sex. It was great. I enjoyed myself. Did you?" Now I turn my gaze toward him.

"Of course I did. But I felt like it was a little rougher than you'd like. And I'm sorry for that."

"You don't need to be." I shoot him a quick smirk over my shoulder.

"So, you enjoyed it?"

"That's what I said, isn't it?"

"I'm sorry, I know I'm repeating myself, but I just want to be sure."

Putting the knife down, I turn to face him and put my hands on his shoulders. "I know that I was a little hesitant to try anything yesterday, but what just happened...I don't know. It opened my eyes...and I liked it. Ten out of ten would do it again."

A wide smile spans his face as he grabs on to my hips and pulls me closer. "Really?"

With tight lips, I nod.

He drops his forehead to mine. "Why are we having so much trouble with this transition?"

"Because it's a big one. We're going from really good friends who know so much about each other in every other aspect of life and have a lot of respect for each other, to lovers who are learning entirely new sides of one another. And maybe don't want to push too much *because* of how well we know each other, since it can change everything instead of just losing a possibility." My eyes widen for a moment as the words pour out of me without much thought, but I realize that it's exactly how I feel.

He nods against my head, his grip on my waist tightening. "I want this to work, Mazie."

"I do too." I stay in his embrace for another moment before pulling away and assembling our sandwiches. He stands right behind me, his chin on my shoulder as I carefully layer the turkey and vegetables.

"Don't forget to add the peppers to yours." The words are murmured against my ear and a small smile pulls up my lips.

Once the tops are on the sandwiches, Zach reaches around me and grabs the plates while I go to the pantry and get out a bag of chips.

We sit in what over the years have become our usual spots at the table. This, this aspect feels normal. Aside from the fact that he's half naked and I'm only wearing one of his t-shirts. Not to mention the sex we just had that has me wincing while I sit.

It's like I said before. We just need a little time to adjust to being romantically involved.

At least, I hope so.

Chapter 14

Zach

Though the weekend started a little rocky, it was amazing to spend it with Mazie. Being with her in such a carefree way, not having to be afraid I might slip up and say or do something I shouldn't, it was freeing.

Never had I realized how much I really held back with her. It was such a subconscious thing that I didn't even realize I was doing it. Until today when I reflect on our time together.

Leaving her this morning was nearly impossible. It wasn't just that I didn't want to come to work—who does on a Monday morning? It was more so that I didn't want to leave *her*. Her warmth, her embrace, her glances.

As I stare up at the sheriff's department, I tighten my grip on my duffel bag, take a deep breath, and walk through the front door. The precinct is small, so it doesn't take me long to bump into Steve.

"Whoa. Take is easy there, killer. We're not all built like you, Zach." He puts a hand on my shoulder to stabilize himself.

"Sorry. Not watching where I'm going."

"You seem...unhappy to be here. You're never unhappy to be here."

"Had a really great weekend. Wasn't quite ready to leave that little nest yet."

"Nest? You were with Mazie, weren't you? About damn time."

My brows pull together, and I stop short. "You too?"

"What do you mean?"

I run a hand through my hair. "It seems everybody except for me and Mazie saw that we had something."

"Seriously? I always thought she was just...turning you down or something." His shoulders lift like it's no big deal.

My chin drops to my chest, and I shake my head. I can't even muster a comeback.

"Well, at least now I can tell Bianca. She'll be thrilled. What does Mazie's brother think about the situation?"

"Uh, I haven't officially told him yet."

"Really? Is that safe? You didn't think to, like, get his permission or whatever?"

I flip the combo on my locker and pull it open. "I don't need his permission to date his sister. I don't think. Whatever, he gave his blessing and was one of the many who apparently saw that we had feelings for each other before we did."

"You know you have to tell him, right?"

The thought gives me pause. "Do I? Or should it come from Mazie?"

"Definitely you. You're fucking his sister." My jaw ticks at the crassness of his statement. "You should be the one to fess up."

"It'll have to wait until I'm off."

"You don't think she'll tell him in the meantime?"

"I have no idea, but I don't have any other choice. It's not a phone conversation, it's a face-to-face one."

"So head over to his place on your rounds." He says it like it's just the easiest thing in the world.

"He's out in Pineville City. Can't do that. Plus, he's at work."

"Oh, right, right." Sometimes I wonder if Steve isn't so bright or just doesn't pay attention to things that don't interest him. Maybe it's a combination of the two. He's a good cop. When he's focused.

But he has me thinking. Am I supposed to be the one to tell Eli that I'm dating Mazie? Will it matter if she tells him first? It's not that I expect it to be a big deal, as he's the one who told me to go for it.

I do suppose it's a courtesy to tell him instead of him just finding out, though. Does he think it's happened already, and I haven't said anything? Shit, what a clusterfuck this is turning into. I run a hand down my face and my palm rubs against a weekend's worth of stubble.

As I change into my uniform, all I can think about is the fact that Mazie's surely telling her sisters. Whether at this very moment, or at some point today, it's going to happen. The Baker clan is going to know about us and get to celebrate that they were all right. I wonder who will win the pool.

There's no way I can get off work today and *not* head to Eli's. It puts a slight damper on my plan of seeing Mazie as soon as possible, but this is important. At least, that's what I'm being led to believe.

By the time lunch rolls around, I haven't been able to stop thinking about it. I need to make sure Eli's free tonight.

Digging in my pocket for my phone, I swipe it open and click his contact, but then my fingers hesitate above the screen.

With a deep breath and shake of my head, I type out the message. I'm being ridiculous. It's just Eli.

Hey man. You around tonight? Want to talk to you about something.

The phone immediately lights up and vibrates in my hand. With a groan, I swipe the green button.

"What's up?"

"You finally started dating my sister. About damn time."

"How did you know?"

"It's been a couple weeks since our late-night chat." He pauses, and I hear the distinct sound of a zipper closing in the background. "And you never text to see if I'm free. We just show up at each other's place. It's almost like a rule."

I'd love to talk about the situation, but the zipper has me distracted. "Are you...are you in the bathroom?"

"Huh? Oh, no." A soft voice sounds in the background, and I strain my ears to hear what's being said.

"I definitely heard a zipper. What's going on?"

"Just having some fun with the professor for intro to sociology." There's a freeness to his voice that's very unlike him.

Enough so that I pull the phone from my ear to double check the contact on screen.

"Hang on a sec." I hear crackle as his hand covers the mouthpiece. "Okay, sorry, just letting her out of my office."

"Are you at work?" The shock is hard to contain. While Eli's not quite as into relationships and monogamy as I am, I've never known him to mess around at work. It makes worry climb up my spine. "Do you need to grab a drink or something? What's going on with you?"

"Don't know what you're talking about. My baby sisters are all getting hitched and starting families. I'm sure as shit not getting any younger. I may as well have a little fun. Especially since it's all I have." The last part comes out mumbled.

"I'm not getting married to your sister, Eli."

"Not yet." He has a point. What the fuck am I doing with Mazie if I don't plan to take it all the way? We're in our thirties, not spring chickens anymore. And there's no point screwing around with her if I don't plan to take it to the next level. It's not fair to either of us.

But we've only been officially together for a weekend.

"Not any time soon. Is that what this is about? You want the family life?" He's never expressed a want to be a family man. With the way he grew up, I kind of always expected it, but he's never flat out said it. Not to mention, I never would have taken him for the type to be jealous of his sisters having it before him.

"I don't know anymore, Zach. I've always wanted it, but it feels harder and harder to come by. And so much further away. There's just been a lot of shit coming up in the past few years with Liv and Alina getting married, and Liv having Jordanna. I'm sure Alina's not far behind. And now you and Mazie."

Silence fills the line, and I don't know what to say. We've been friends for decades, but we've never been overly emotional.

But he solves the problem for me. "Anyway, whatever. I was lonely, she was there, she offered, I took her up on it. One-time thing. We're both consenting adults, so who gives a fuck."

"I'm just surprised, is all." I try to keep the judgment out of my voice. It's clear that's not what he's seeking.

"Listen, I'd love to shoot the shit or whatever, but I have class in about twenty on the other side of campus. I already gave you my go ahead to be with Mazie, and shared my shock that it took so long, so thanks for the courtesy call? That's what this is. Right?"

"Busted. I wanted to make sure you heard it from me and not the Juniper Grove gossip mill or the sisters."

"Appreciate that, man. Later."

Without another word, he hangs up. Well, that went...interestingly. It's not like I was expecting much of a conversation, or any sort of beratement, but the girl in his office was far from my list.

I guess the best thing to take from this is that he knows and seems completely comfortable with it. Some of the rest is a bit concerning, but I'll be sure to carve out some time for him in the next week to find out what exactly his gripe is.

Chapter 15
Mazie

It's not until after lunch that I can bolster myself up to go to the café. There isn't anything I need to do there today, besides talk to my sisters.

Though Zach and I didn't exactly discuss it, I'm sure telling them is fine.

Going in now will work perfectly. The lunch rush should be wrapping up, and it'll be quiet for us to chat.

Thankfully, walking in, I see that it's completely empty except for Liv, who's standing behind the counter, wiping a rag across it. Her eyes lift as the bell above my head chimes and her eyes widen.

"Oh my God, it finally happened. You and Zach had sex. Alina! Get out here!"

"How did you—"

"Okay, what's the emergency?" Alina looks over at me when Liv juts her chin in my direction. Her jaw drops before she starts jumping up and down, clapping her hands. "It finally happened!"

"That's what I said." Liv jabs her in the side with her elbow.

I give my head a quick shake. "How can you tell?"

"Oh good, she's not denying it." Alina and Liv share a quick look before glancing back at me.

I raise a hand to my face, covering my eyes, while the other hand plants on my hip. I nearly jump out of my skin when I feel two sets of arms wrapping around me on either side. I hadn't heard them leave the counter.

"We love you, Maze. And we're happy for you."

"How could you tell?" Do I have a giant neon 'recently had sex with her best friend' sign above my head that only other people can see?

"We're your sisters. We know you. And you're practically glowing brightly enough to combat the sun." Liv swoops some curls over my shoulder. Ones that are fresh and curly after the rat's nest they were from this weekend.

"Besides, at one point in time, you shared that kind of information with us. Maybe not quite as vocally as Liv"—Alina and I look at her, and she just shrugs—"but we learned the signs."

"I have *recently had sex* signs?" My face burns at the thought. Maybe I should have just stayed home.

"Subtle ones. That only we, as your siblings, would notice." Sometimes I swear Liv can read my mind.

"Like what?" Now I need to know. I want to keep myself aware of them so that I can maybe control them.

"You hold your shoulders back a little more."

"And your chin a little higher."

"Your eyes literally sparkle."

"Your lips look more plump."

"And the smile," they say in unison.

"I smile a lot. Don't I?" One corner of my mouth tips down as I consider.

"This one is different. You don't exactly have resting bitch face. After you've had sex, or at least what I can tell is good sex, your lips are quirked up and you just look...happy." Liv gives me a quick once-over before nodding, like she's pleased with her assessment.

But my brows pull together. "Do I not look happy most of the time?"

Now they exchange another glance, this one heavier. My chest flutters as I wait for one of them to speak.

"You look stressed. And honestly, a bit depressed." Alina pulls her lower lip between her teeth.

I never realized that my emotions showed through that clearly. In fact, I was pretty sure I did a good job of hiding them. From everybody. Eli's always been able to see right through me, but he's overly perceptive with all three of us. Part of me just assumed it was a little bit of his personality, a little bit of being the oldest and watching us all grow up.

Now I wonder if they can see when I'm struggling more often than not.

"Okay. Now that we know what happened, we want more." Liv's like a giddy schoolgirl, ready to hear all the juicy gossip.

"I'm *not* giving you details." That's never been my thing.

"That's not what she means. We know you're not like that. But it's you and Zach. We've all been expecting this for...well...forever."

I roll my eyes. "A little over dramatic. Don't you think?"

They both shrug. "But not wrong." Liv squeezes my shoulder before skipping away and heading straight to the espresso machine.

As far as she's concerned, what good is some gossip without caffeine to go with it?

Alina and I find a table, and I immediately fold my hands together on the wooden surface. Liv sits a few moments later, depositing three coffees in front of us. Though my preferences tend to change every now and again, I do have a somewhat regular order of a vanilla latte. The quick sip I take confirms that this is what she made for me.

"Alright. Spill." Liv scooches back in her chair, lounging comfortable while she sips her coffee.

"I'm not sure what you want to know, exactly."

"Well, the last we had heard from you about the situation, he had kissed you. And then basically ignored you for two weeks."

"I wouldn't exactly say he *ignored* me. We just...didn't talk as much as usual." Saying that he ignored me feels extreme. We all need space sometimes. And that's what he was trying to give me. I understand it, but I'm not sure they would.

"Whatever happened. We want to know how things went from not talking to sex."

"It was Friday, and I hadn't heard from him and was shocked when he showed up at my door for movie night, complete with snacks." As though planned, at the same time, they both lean forward in their chairs and wrap both hands around their cups.

"At a certain point, I had to call attention to what happened. Especially because he was acting like *nothing* happened, and I couldn't stop thinking about it." I tuck a curl behind my ear and look down at the table. "And after we talked a little, cleared the air or whatever, he just grabbed me and yanked me into his lap and kissed me again. Only this time, I didn't stop him."

They both stare at me with wide eyes, like they're expecting more. But there's nothing else I'm willing to give them.

"Was it just a one-time thing?" Liv cocks an eyebrow.

"He spent the weekend." I don't need to share about the six times we had sex in that short window.

"Alright. We get it. Not much for the details. But at least tell us this. How was it?"

A wide smile pulls at my lips as my face heats. "Incredible." Butterflies take flight in my stomach as I think about our times together. Even the roughness grew on me in just a few short hours. It's like Zach knows exactly how to use his body to pleasure mine. Things I thought I'd never be up for I now find myself craving.

If things had been different, if I hadn't had to go into mom mode when I did, maybe I'd be willing to have that sisterly girl talk and give them *some* more intimate details.

It's one small reason why I didn't keep many friends after my parents passed away. Not only was I busy raising my little sisters, but I didn't want to gossip and partake in the talk about our sex lives. The few friends I had just assumed I wasn't having any, and that was good enough for me. But to them, I became boring. No longer was I the fun friend who would know about all the best parties because of her older brother.

Alina's hand covering mine pulls me from my distant thoughts. "We're happy for you, Maze. Especially if you're happy. Are you?" She ducks her head so her eyes can meet mine.

"So far, yeah. I don't know how I was so blind to it for so long. It's just...we click."

Liv giggles. "That's what we've been trying to tell you! I always kind of took your word for it, assumed you two had some sort of chat or tried it once and it didn't go well. But Jameson was so sure there was something there, at least on Zach's side. I started paying closer attention after that. He was definitely right."

"You all were." Defeat drips from my words as my shoulders slump. How blind I was.

"How does Eli feel about it?" Alina bites her lip as she thinks about it.

"Honestly, I'm not sure. He's never expressed any issue with it. But I haven't talked to him yet."

"Zach's his best friend." I'm not sure why Liv feels the need to point this out.

"Zach's *my* best friend."

"Whatever. You basically share him. But I don't know, that might be weird for Eli?"

While I hadn't really given it much thought, now the worry starts to creep up my spine and wiggle into my mind. Is Eli going to be mad? Hurt? Disappointed? I honestly can't imagine him feeling any of those things if I'm happy, but it is Zach. They've been friends for over twenty years. Maybe it's a problem he didn't even know he'd have until it happened.

Either way, I'm going to have to have a visit with my big brother. And soon.

Chapter 16
Zach

The week has flown by, and my time with Mazie has been nothing short of amazing. She's relaxed a lot more, and we've fallen into a sort of routine. While my shifts can vary both in start time and length, Mazie's an early riser, up by seven every single morning.

Even though she's happy to let me sleep in while she gets the day started with coffee and whipping up breakfast, I often get up as well. Most days, I try to start with a quick run before breakfast is served.

I text her before I leave the precinct, so she knows I'm on my way back, and after dinner, I insist on at least helping clean up. Once that's finished, we settle on the couch for a show or movie. It's comfortable and it's easy.

Which is why when Mazie seems a little out of sorts this morning, worry weighs down my features. She's in a bit of a tizzy, clearly anxious about something, but what I can't quite place.

The doors and windows were all locked last night, I made sure of it. I helped her pull the curtains shut. So I can't imagine what has her pacing the kitchen and mumbling to herself, but I opt to skip my run today because of it.

After twenty minutes of watching her ping around the kitchen, I walk over to her and put my hands on her shoulders, dipping my head to meet her gaze. Her fingers are threaded together, her sapphire eyes are wide.

"M. What's going on?" Concern laces my voice. Maybe I've fallen into a false sense of security, and she actually wants to break up. Despite my three day "marriage" in first grade, it'd be the shortest relationship I've ever had.

"Nothing. What do you mean?" She twists her fingers, and her eyes dart around the room.

"Something's bothering you. What is it?" I rub my hands down her arms and back up again.

"It's just..." She takes a deep breath and stops talking.

I look at her with my brows high, urging her to continue.

A heavy sigh makes her head droop. "I know it's been like a week, but you're here all the time anyway, and I like having you here and want you here as much as possible. I wanted to give you a key, but you already have one. So I was worrying about how to give you something you already have, or just telling you to use it so I can keep the door locked, and then I started thinking about how fast it is and that maybe you're not there yet." She pulls her bottom lip between her teeth as she lifts her gaze to mine.

I tug her into my chest, wrapping my arms around her shoulders and tucking her head under my chin. "Next time, just bring it up. Don't overthink it."

She pulls back to look at me. "That's kind of what I do. You should know that by now."

With a shake of my head, I push her ear back against my chest. "I just mean, there's no reason to hold anything back from me. And while it may seem quick in terms of the relationship, things are different than normal. We've been close friends for so long that we don't have to lay as much groundwork. In a lot of ways, the only thing that's changed is the amount of time we spend together and the fact that we have really awesome sex."

Her body shakes with a light laugh, but she remains silent.

"I didn't know that having the door unlocked for me was bothering you. I wish you had said something. I don't mind using my key, and don't need some grand gesture of you giving it to me because we're in a relationship. I know we haven't been to my apartment yet, but I'd hope if we're ever there, or I'm there and you're coming over, that you'd feel free to use *your* spare key to let yourself in."

Though she nods against my chest, there's still a tightness to her body. "What else is bothering you?"

Her shoulders slump, and she relaxes against me. I'm not sure if it was some sort of test that I happily passed, or if she was just reluctant to share. "Eli's coming by the café today."

My brow furrows, and now I'm seven shades of confused. She and Eli are thick as thieves. They've always been super close. I'm not sure why his presence would put her into such a mood.

As though reading my mind, she continues. "We're going to talk about us. You and me."

"I mean, he already knows. I told him. And he seems fine with it." We had discussed my phone call the night it happened. She was equally as concerned about the sociology professor.

"Yeah, but you're the friend, not the sister. You know he's always been protective of the three of us."

"He's your brother, that's his job. But I don't think it's going to be bad, M."

"I know. And the rational part of my brain doesn't either. But then there's the irrational part that worries he's going to make me choose or be angry or some other unlikely situation."

I tighten my arms around her and press my lips to the top of her head. "You know he's not going to do that. In his eyes, you can do no wrong." I'm pretty sure none of them can.

"Maybe that's how it looks from the outside, but if anybody can be a fuckup in Eli's eyes, it's me."

While I'm closer to the family than most, I don't actually know the inner workings of the Bakers. Though I'd bet it's more that Eli just holds Mazie to higher standards than the younger sisters because she took on the role of a mom and had more time with their parents to learn how to be a good person.

"Do you want me to go with you? Intervene and talk to him first?"

"No. This needs to be a sibling discussion. And like I said, some part of me is sure it's going to be just fine. But there's that tiny little part that says, 'what if it's not?' And right now, that part is winning."

I'd never pretend to know what goes on in Mazie's head or what it's like to deal with day in and day out. But she spends a lot of time warring with herself and worrying about things that take more of her energy than necessary. As much as I wish my presence and support would change that, the reasons are rooted deep in her psyche.

"When are you supposed to be meeting him?"

"I figured I'd leave with you, so soon. He has class at like ten or something, so he said he'd swing out this way first, grab some breakfast at the café."

My eyes flick to the clock on the stove. It's a quarter after seven, which means I have to leave in about a half hour to make it to the precinct in time to start my shift.

"How about we leave in twenty and I drive you? I'll also grab breakfast at the café."

"You don't have to do that." Her actions betray her words as she buries into my chest.

Her shoulders dip once more, and she pulls from my embrace after I press a kiss to her head. "We should get ready."

She's dressed and anxiously sitting on the edge of the bed, her knee bouncing incessantly by the time I get out of my quick shower. While I want to give her more comfort, there's nothing I can say or do in this instance, and that she just has to live through the chat with Eli to see that it's not as terrible as she fears.

"I'll drive you there, but I won't be able to bring you back. Do you want to take two cars?" I'm worried about her focus right now. Not that it's far, and not that she's likely to encounter much of, well, anything. But it only takes one extra person on the road and her inability to pay close attention to her surroundings.

"That's okay. Eli can bring me back. Or one of the girls." Her mind seems to be in the same place as mine.

I stand behind her on the front step as she locks, checks, and then rechecks the door before I open the passenger side door for her. She gives me a tight smile as she lowers herself into the car, pulling her purse into her lap. It's moments like this when I feel utterly helpless with Mazie. They're not new, but now it's compounded. There's more to it. The need to save her from herself is stronger.

The second I'm in the car, I link my fingers with hers and pull the back of her hand to my mouth before resting them on the center console. It only takes five minutes to get to Three Sticks, and as she looks through the picture window into the café, her body relaxes at the sight of her sister. Liv's moving around the open space freely, getting things ready for the morning or perhaps cleaning up from the early customers.

Walking around to Mazie's side, I open her door and extend a hand. With a deep breath, she exits the car. A smile spans her face as we walk through the door, the tiny bell above us announcing our entrance.

Liv's pink streaks whip through the air as she spins around to see who entered. A brief look of confusion crosses her face before a wide smile. "Hey, Zee. Were we expecting you today?"

"Probably not, Bibly." Their nicknames have always been...interesting. And at times confusing to keep up with. But it's very much a part of the Bakers. "Eli's swinging by shortly so he and I can chat."

"Oh cool. It's been a minute since I've seen big bro. Think I have time to call Jameson to swing by with Jordanna?" She's already moving behind the counter and pulling out her purse.

"Can't hurt."

After Liv shoots off a quick text, she raises her gaze back up, spreading her hands as she leans against the counter. "What can I get you guys this morning? Coppuccino for you, Zach?" She winks.

"You know I hate that you guys call it that."

"And *you* know we like the cutesy names. I mean, Alina made one up for her and Cam." She waves her hand at the board above her head.

Mazie turns to face me and rests her hand against my chest. "You were the first one to order a cappuccino. And really, our first customer. It only felt right to name it after you. Plus, it's just a fun play on words for us."

"It's better than Jameson's!" Liv calls over her shoulder while she works the machine.

I give a moment of consideration before I realize that it could, in fact, be worse, as his is a Diva Espresso. Though Jameson's wasn't named after him.

Unfortunately, I haven't had much time to get to know him. Between work, and the two of them having Jordanna, it's been too crazy to take the time. Plus, I'm not exactly family or anybody of importance besides Mazie and Eli's friend. At least, I wasn't.

Jameson's a good guy, the little I've chatted with him. But he's a bit intimidating. He probably shouldn't be, as we're the same age, roughly the same height. It's more his put together, big city guy attitude. Not just that, but he was able to tame Liv and win over Mazie. Neither of which are easy feats.

"Anything else today, Zach?" Liv's voice pulls me back into focus.

My brows furrow at the bag next to my to-go coffee. "What's in the bag?"

"Coffee cake muffin."

My eyes widen and my mouth waters. Nothing's better than Alina's coffee cake muffins. "You're my favorite little sister. Did you know that?"

"Hey! I heard that!" Alina bellows as the door to the kitchen swings open and she walks out with her hands on her hips, flour on her cheek and in her hair.

"I was just saying that 'cause she was here and you weren't. Can't have my favorite muffin without the wonderful chef who created them, can I?" I shoot a wink her way, and she rolls her eyes.

It's easy to fit in with the girls who have been like baby sisters to me for most of my life. Their spouses may be a different story. I'll be the first to admit that I may judge Cameron a little harshly for his past. Maybe it's the cop in me, or maybe it's that he hurt Alina and I saw the devastation.

"Sorry, ladies, I'd love to stay and chat, but I have to get to work." I turn to Mazie and lower my head so only she can hear me. "I'll see you later. Okay? No stressing. It's going to be fine. I promise."

Her fingers twist into my shirt as she nods. I dip my head to meet her lips, then press another kiss to her forehead before heading for the door.

"Aw, you guys are so cute." It's the last thing I hear as I walk through the door, and it brings a smile to my face.

It may have started off on the wrong foot, but today's going to be a good day.

Chapter 17
Mazie

T he warmth from Zach's kiss quickly fades as I think about the conversation that lies ahead. He's right, my sisters are right. It's just Eli. Nothing bad is going to happen. But I can't help stressing. It's in my nature.

Every time the bell chimes, my head snaps up from looking down at my feet where I stand behind the counter.

The first time it was a customer that Liv promptly and cheerily helped. The second time it was Jameson and Jordanna. She's gotten so big; I feel like I've been a neglectful aunt. While it's only been a couple of weeks since I visited with her, a lot changed in those few days.

Jameson puts her down the second they're through the door and Liv rounds the counter. The smiles that span all of their faces are infectious. Jordanna puts her chubby little arms out, saying "Mama" as she toddles toward Liv, who's squatting on the floor.

"There's my sweet girl." Liv scoops her happy little toddler into her arms and kisses all over her face.

"She's been asking for mama since you left this morning." Jameson plants his hands on his hips and looks at Jordanna with endearment, mixed with a little bit of frustration.

"You want to go see Auntie Mazie?" Liv turns toward me and tilts Jordanna in my direction, but she throws her arms around Liv's neck.

"No. Mama."

"How about Auntie Lina?" Alina takes a step forward with a giant smile on her face and arms outstretched.

"No. Mama."

"Don't be too upset about it, ladies. She's just in a mama-centric mood. Watch. Jordanna, want to come see Dada?" Jameson stretches his arms wide, smiles, and nods at his daughter.

Who turns away from him and buries into Liv's shoulder. "No. Mama."

Jameson sighs and runs a hand through his hair. "Okay. Time for another one."

"Jameson!" Liv practically shrieks.

"What? I need at least one who loves me."

"Oh my God, you're being so dramatic. Jordanna loves you." She pulls the little girl from her chest and tickles her belly. "Right? You love Dada."

Jordanna's tiny giggles fill the café, and we all smile.

"She just loves Mama more." Liv sticks her tongue out at Jameson, who rolls his eyes, and runs a hand down his face.

The whole exchange has me feeling lighter. Until the door chimes and Eli waltzes through.

Everybody turns to the door, and Jordanna shows where her true love lies as she reaches for my brother. "LiLi! LiLi!"

"Well, there's my favorite girl in the whole world!" Eli scoops her into his arms, and she snuggles into his shoulder. It's his uncanny ability to blend in with everybody. I sometimes wonder if there's anybody in the world who wouldn't love Eli.

My stomach drops when his eyes lock on mine.

But he smiles warmly and shoots me a wink. He probably knows I'm overthinking, because that's just how he is.

Jordanna leans back and hits Eli in the face with her tiny hands. "Mama, Mama."

"You know, I do kind of look like your mama." While our features are all different, put any one of us next to another and you can see a strong resemblance. Liv's hair has the pink, mine has a bit more of a reddish hue to it, but all four of us have shades of brown, just like Mom did. The curls come from Dad, as do the variations in blue eye color.

"Mama, Mama." She keeps hitting Eli in the face, who takes it in stride and smiles despite what's surely tiny wet hands.

"Oh, you want to go to Mama?"

"Yeth." She gives a tiny nod but doesn't take her eyes from Eli.

"Okay then. Should we fly?"

She bounces in Eli's hold and her tiny hands hit against his chest. "Fy! Fy!"

He tips her forward, supporting her under her chest and legs as he flies her around the café before bringing her to Liv, whose smile makes my heart warm. She's an amazing mother. The thought brings tears to my eyes, because I know how much Mom and Dad would love to see this. To see their baby being a parent, and such a good one.

"Coffee?" Liv looks up at Eli as she holds Jordanna's back against her chest.

"Yeah. Please. And a muffin."

"What kind?"

"Surprise me." While the rest of us have favorites, Eli really doesn't. Or if he has one, he's never let any of us know. He's like that with so many things.

He and I may be the closest in the sibling group, but there are still so many things he keeps from me. Sometimes I feel like I know my brother so well. Other times, he feels like a complete mystery to me.

With a smirk on his face, he walks over and throws his arm over my shoulder as he guides me toward a table. "So. You're finally dating my best friend?"

I glance up at him with an eyebrow raised. "Sorry, but he's *my* best friend."

He lifts a shoulder and pulls out a chair for me. "Eh. He was mine first."

"Would you like him back?"

"Nah." He waves a hand through the air. "He's all yours."

I open my mouth to ask a question—what, I'm not really sure—when Liv comes over with Eli's coffee and a mixed berry muffin. I know they're her favorite.

He smiles up at her before grabbing a big piece and shoveling it in his mouth. "Thanks, babiest sis."

Liv pats him on the shoulder as she walks away, leaving us in silence once again.

But this time, instead of trying to say something, I chew the inside of my cheek. For some reason, it's like I've forgotten how to have a conversation with my brother.

"Hey."

My gaze darts over to his.

Eli shakes his head with his brows drawn together. "What gives? Why are you being weird?"

"I just...I don't know. Are you, like, mad that I'm dating Zach?"

"Why in the world would I be mad? We've all thought it was going to take some sort of life-altering event to make you realize that there was something between you two."

"I don't know. Isn't it against some sort of like rules or something to date your brother's friend? Or your friend's sister?"

He waves a hand through the air again as he takes a sip of his coffee. "When have I ever cared about so-called rules? Besides, when it's meant to be, it's meant to be. And you and Zach have been circling each other, completely blind to the attraction you two had for far too long. Any objections I could have had are long since passed."

My cheeks heat. "You think we're meant to be?"

Eli pauses mid-bite and looks up at me through his lashes. "Do you not?"

I start picking at my nails. "I'm not sure. It's only been a week. It feels too soon to make such a distinction."

"Maybe it's been a week of *officially* dating, but let's be real. There's been so much between you two for years that you don't need those early parts of the relationship to get to know each other. You already do. You have the foundation most have to build first. Besides, Mom and Dad got married after only knowing each other for six months." That's one change in Eli, and with some help, now me. We can both say "Mom" and "Dad" with ease, where it's still a bit of a struggle for Alina and Liv.

"I forgot about that." While my parents may not have known each other long, they were madly in love. All the way up to their death. They showed us what a solid relationship and partnership looked like.

They never shied away from being affectionate around us. Dad always held Mom's hand in the car and any time they weren't each holding one of ours when we were out somewhere. Sometimes when a certain song played on the radio or in a movie we were watching, Dad would take Mom in his arms and dance around the living room. They complimented each other. They were always a team, a united front.

"You and Zach certainly know each other more than the vast majority of people who start a relationship together. I mean, shit, the last girl I was in a relationship with...well...let's just leave it at you and Zach would have found the others crazy by now."

My eyes narrow. "Oh yeah. Speaking of. What's up with the sociology professor in your office the other day?" I cock my head to the side as I take him in.

He flops back in his chair and rolls his eyes. "Zach told you? Sheesh, maybe I *don't* want you two dating." His fingers pick at his muffin. That only makes me more concerned.

"What's going on, Eli?"

"Nothing. Can't a guy have a little fun? All his little sisters are getting married and—"

"I'm not getting married."

"Yet." Our eyes lock, and I see how serious he is. He really thinks this is going all the way. It's a thought I haven't allowed myself to have yet. While I typically don't want to waste time in a relationship that I see going nowhere, it's hard to see such an end game so soon. Plus, Zach's different.

Eli's right, we have the history, the foundation. Marriage just seems...fast.

"Either way. I was just having some fun. Consenting adults and all that. Besides, how else am I going to find somebody to be with?"

"Do you always lead with sex?" I raise an eyebrow, knowing he not only doesn't operate that way, but that it's far outside of the realm of how we were raised. Sometimes, I think Eli's still going through his rebellious stage, just a little later in life and rebelling against ghosts.

"When it's convenient. Which in this case, it was." He sighs heavily and his shoulders droop. "Listen, I don't need your concern. Or Zach's. I'm fine. Just been in a bit of a dry spell and having some feelings about being the oldest, yet last Baker to find somebody." His eyebrows crunch together, and he picks at his cup.

Most people don't know this, and Liv and Alina were too young to remember. But as much as I'd play with my dolls and pretend to be a mom, Eli would do the same but pretend to be a dad. I know one of his goals in life is to emulate Dad, to be the partner he was and the father he was. But I didn't know he was worried about not having that.

"Eli, I—"

He flicks his watch out and quickly stands, nearly knocking his chair over. "Shit. I gotta go. I'm just barely going to make it to class on time. Doesn't look good when the professor is late."

Before I've even had a chance to get up, he's rounded the table and wrapped his arm around my shoulders. "I love you. I'm happy for you and Zach. Stop worrying about me."

"I love you too. But it's kind of what I do. About as easily as I breathe."

He rolls his eyes and ruffles my hair, just like he did when we were kids. "I'm perfectly fine, Mae."

"If you say so. Don't be a stranger. Been a while since we've seen you."

"I was just at Liv's a few days ago. But I'm wrapping up class for the summer, then I'll be in your hair for a few weeks before summer classes start." His hands are up on either side as he backs through the café. He gives Liv and Alina a quick hug each, a small kiss to Jordanna, and he and Jameson do that weird man-hug thing I've never understood.

Then he's gone, and the café feels smaller, duller. Eli brings that brightness and fullness with him everywhere he goes.

He was destined for so much more. His students truly have no idea how lucky they are to have him.

Chapter 18

Zach

The conversation with Eli seemed to go as well as I thought it would. By the time I got to Mazie's that night, she was humming in the kitchen while getting dinner together. When I asked how it went, she beamed up at me.

My biggest problem since then is that I haven't had a day off to spend with Mazie. It's not quite the same, only seeing her at night and in the morning. Our routine is consistent, and I know that puts her in a comfortable place since it's predictable, but one of us ends up falling asleep on the couch every night by nine o'clock. We're already an old married couple and we've only been dating for a couple of weeks.

While it doesn't quite bode well for our future, it's also not that surprising. Neither of us are really the type to want to go out, except maybe to dinner, which I haven't had the time for yet.

It's why I'm so excited to have Friday off. Not just because it's movie night again, but because we have the entire day together.

I swung by the store yesterday on my way back to her place to grab the required movie snacks. While we still have yet to complete a scary movie,

I plan to let it be her turn to pick something that I'll surely regret having to sit through.

If I'm lucky, we won't really end up watching that much anyway. In fact, part of me is considering doing an entire movie day. Just the two of us, relaxing on the couch, no interruptions. The girls have the café and rarely need Mazie's input on anything, which is why she works from home so much. She can put off any phone calls, orders, or anything else until Monday.

I'd love to be the one who makes her breakfast and lets her sleep in, but we both decided it was probably better if I stuck to grilling, at least for a while. Though Jenna tried to include me and Eli in the crafting of meals, it often went over our heads. In fact, I'm pretty sure it wasn't really something any of the Bakers enjoyed except Alina.

With my job, it's easier to just grab something quick or make something easy. The most home-cooked meals I have are when I'm at Mazie's or invited to Baker Sunday dinner.

I heave a sigh and Mazie stirs in her spot sprawled across my chest. She fell asleep about an hour ago, but I just haven't been able to shut my brain off.

She turns to look at me, her sapphire eyes blinking slowly, and a smile creeps across her lips. "What are you doing awake?"

I tuck a curl behind her ear and shrug. "Can't sleep."

"Anything you want to talk about?"

"No. Just excited about tomorrow. How would you feel about movie *day* instead of movie night?" My brows raise as I pose the question, trailing my fingertips down her back.

"That sounds fun. But whose turn is it?"

A small laugh breaks through my lips and I hang my head. "I figured we could take turns."

"You know, we've had to start two scary movies and not a single romcom. I'm not sure that's fair."

"The keyword here is *start*. We haven't finished any." Every part of me is planning to let her watch as many romcoms as she wants. But it's fun to tease.

She turns her face against my chest and groans before looking back at me, a twinkle skittering through her eyes.

Reaching forward, I grip the back of her neck at the same time I loop my other arm around her waist and pull her mouth to mine. Her body glides over mine as I sweep my tongue through her lips.

I keep my hold on her neck, twisting my fingers into her auburn locks as my other hand trails down her back and over her ass so my fingers can graze her pussy.

She pulls away, resting her fingers lightly on my chest. "I'm on my period."

"So?"

Her brows bunch, and she pushes a little further away. "Um. I'm bleeding?" She says it like she's not sure I understand.

"I get that. Do you care?"

"Well, no. But I thought you would."

"Why would I?"

"Because...it's kind of gross?"

"It's entirely natural, and it doesn't bother me. Any other objections?"

"No."

I smack her ass...hard. "Good. Then get your fine ass in the fucking shower."

Slowly, she climbs off of me and gets off the bed, looking back in my general direction over her shoulder as she walks toward the bathroom.

"I'll give you a second to do whatever you need to do to be ready for me and I'll join you in the shower. Unless you don't want to?" I raise an eyebrow as I look at her, but a smile creeps across her face as she skips into the bathroom.

A second later, the shower's on but I give her a minute. It's not until she yells "Are you coming?" that I jump out of bed.

Her curls are piled in a messy bun on the very top of her head. I know it's her way of showing she doesn't want to get her hair wet. Which is too bad, really, because I love to twist it around my hand.

Taking an extra minute, I stand and watch as rivulets of water dash down her incredible body. My cock bobs in front of me, and I take it in my hand, gliding up and down my length while she stands with her eyes closed and head tipped up under the flow of water.

"Are you going to join me?" One of her eyes pops open as she turns to look at me.

"Just enjoying this image."

"Well, I'm pretty sure it's more enjoyable from this side of the glass. At least, I'd have to assume." The bit of shyness that she first exhibited has long since passed.

I step into the shower, standing in the stream in front of her as I place my palms on her thighs and trail them up her slick body. Her luscious curves make my dick painfully hard.

Gripping her by the neck, I push her against the wall, a hiss bleeding through her lips as her back hits the tile. She arches away from the cold sensation, her breasts brushing my chest.

I keep my hand on her throat as I bend and pull her hardened nipple into my mouth.

Her hands hook around my shoulders, one twisting into my hair while the other scratches nails across my shoulder. She moans and lifts her leg to wrap it around my waist.

Starting at her ankle, I glide my fingers up her leg until I reach her thigh, sliding my hand between our bodies to feel her soaking pussy.

With a pop, I release her nipple and my forehead falls against the cool tile. "Fuck, M."

I plunge my fingers inside her, and she claws at my skin, grinding her pelvis toward mine as her head tips toward the ceiling and a moan tears from her lips. Not wanting to waste a second, I hook my fingers, and she practically goes limp in my hold. A quick adjustment has me gripping her ass firmly in my palm while I support her weight and continue to move my fingers.

She bucks against my hand, her body trembling as her fingers yank at my hair just before a gush hits my leg.

I nip at her neck once she stills. "It's so fucking sexy when you do that."

With a groan, I'm lined up to dive into her, but she presses a palm against my chest. "Are you sure?"

My brows pull together. "I just had my fingers inside you."

"Yeah, but you can wash your hands."

"I can wash my dick too, baby."

She rolls her eyes and glances down before meeting mine. "I know. It just...it seems different. I just don't want you to be grossed out."

Raising an eyebrow, I thrust all the way into her, a scream filling the room and bouncing off the tiles.

"Do you know how amazing you feel, Mazie? A little blood isn't going to scare me away."

She nods as her mouth hangs open and her eyes flutter closed. "Good."

One corner of my mouth ticks up as I slide out, leaving just the tip of my cock nestled inside her. Then I slam back into her as her chest heaves. "You like when I fuck you, don't you, baby?"

Her eyes stay pressed together as I move in and out of her. "Oh my God. So much."

The more I thrust, the slipperier the floor seems to get. But I'll be damned if I drop this woman or fall over. Instead, I hasten my pace and hold her ass in both hands.

One thing I hadn't taken into account is the lack of traction on the floor. Unfortunately, that means this is going to go much faster than I want it to. Though, it always does. I'd spend hours upon hours just enjoying Mazie's body.

She's always quick to respond to me, and she's already breathing heavily and trembling in my hold. When her legs tighten around my waist and her pussy clamps down on my cock, trying to move inside her is like what I imagine it'd be to try to move through quicksand. It's nearly impossible, she's so damn tight. It's why a few seconds later, I choke on a breath and come deep inside her while my forehead drops to hers.

Droplets of water fall from the few strands of hair stuck between us at the top of my head. Staring down her torso, I'm transfixed by the place where our bodies meet.

We were blind to it, but it's crystal clear we were meant to be something.

"Sorry, it was quick. I was slipping."

"Not every time has to be a marathon, Zach."

"I just want to make sure you're satisfied first." Putting her needs before my own is easy.

"That doesn't mean it needs to go on and on. You're always good at anticipating my needs, of taking care of me. In every way possible." Her hand trails down my chest, and I gently set her down, guiding her under the stream. The moment the warm water patters against her skin, her head tips against my shoulder.

A hum vibrates against my chest, and I wrap my arms around her middle, pressing a kiss to her temple.

"This is nice. Even if it is the middle of the night." She tips her face up and stands on her toes to brush her lips against my jaw.

Reaching around her, while still keeping her in the water, I grab the bar of soap and lather it between my hands, running them down her chest and over her stomach. My fingers dip between her thighs. It takes all of my self-control not to circle her clit. I soap the joints where her legs meet her hips before letting go and soaping myself up.

After a quick rinse, I climb out of the shower, grabbing a fuzzy blue towel from the closet before getting a red one out for Mazie.

She stands under the stream for another moment, eyes closed as she enjoys the warm liquid pouring over her body before she sighs and turns off the water. Holding the towel out for her, I wrap it around her and run my hands up and down her arms.

"I'm going to step out to give you privacy." Slipping out of the bathroom, I pull on a pair of boxers and settle under the covers.

Mazie comes out just a few minutes later and quickly pulls one of my t-shirts from the drawer, tugging it over her head and scurrying next to me.

Her head nuzzles on my chest, and I press my mouth to the top of her head.

Within moments, her breaths are slow and steady. I'm sure she's asleep when she twitches lightly.

Knowing she's peaceful, that tomorrow is a whole day for just us, I get comfortable with an arm behind my head and close my eyes for the first time all night.

Chapter 19
Mazie

It's been quite a few weeks since Zach and I finally took the step to be more than just friends. And our time together has been nothing but incredible. He's had to work a few night shifts, which leaves me feeling lonely in a way I didn't know was possible. It feels silly, having been single for years.

But I've become not only used to his company, but overly comfortable with it. Not just his presence but the warmth he gives off, the way he wraps around me. The safety I feel in his arms. I'm slightly convinced that the nights we're together are some of the best sleep I've had in years.

It leaves me excited to go to therapy, which is the first time in almost two months. I've worked down to one session a month, unless I'm going through a crisis of some sort, but last month, my therapist was on vacation, and I didn't want to bother her with moving my schedule. Not to mention, I didn't want to take the time from somebody else who needed to see her. I was sure I'd be fine. And I have been.

Sitting in her office brings me a sense of peace. There are some things that I prefer not to relive about my time here and what I've talked about, but overall, it's been helpful.

"Tell me what's been new in your life." Dr. Raylinsky sits in her padded chair, across from the sofa I'm on, with one leg crossed over the other.

"Well, Zach and I are dating. It's been a few weeks now, and things are moving along smoothly. Everything's been great. He practically lives at my house, which I feel like should be weird because it's been such a short time, but it's not strange at all. In fact, it feels really right." I loop a curl behind my ear. Sometimes I get a little overzealous and say too much too fast and need to take a second to breathe. It's something Dr. Raylinsky has taught me in the past.

"And how much time do you spend at his place?" She cants her head to the side as she asks.

"Um. None."

"Why not?"

My brow furrows in confusion. "I mean, everybody would prefer to be at their own home with their belongings. Right?"

"Zach isn't. He seems to be making the compromise to be *away* from his things for you."

I'd never thought about it that way. Sure, there have been a few times I've felt guilty that we're always at my house, but he's never seemed to mind.

"And how often are you getting to the café?" Her eyes narrow as she looks down her nose at me. This question comes up almost every session.

I run a hand up my arm, not loving the direction this conversation is going. "Um, every now and again. I still do most of the work from home."

Dr. Raylinsky nods a few times before bringing her steepled fingers to her pursed lips. "I'm going to suggest something you're not going to like."

My stomach flips. "Okay."

"I want you to spend more time at the café. As many days as you can."

"Why?" A lump has settled in my throat.

"Because I'm worried that you're moving backward and not forward. That you're one meltdown away from becoming completely agoraphobic." While I understand where she's coming from, it seems a little extreme.

"But...it's tourist season."

"All the better."

My eyes widen and my heart races.

"Mazie, you're *safe* at work. It's a safe space for you. It's *your* space. You own it. Your sisters are there. It's probably the second safest and well-known space to you after your home."

"There's...there's just so many people." I swallow harshly.

"I'm not asking you to engage with them. Yet. I'm just asking you to be there more often. Even if you start by being squirreled away in your office. After a few days, I want you to spend ten minutes out on the café floor. Then slowly increase that time until you can be an actual part of the business."

"I do all the backend stuff. I make sure our supplies are kept up." Even as I say it, it sounds weak and unimportant. Liv and Alina could certainly do the added tasks and not bat an eyelash.

"I know, and I understand the importance of that. But think about how hard your sisters work, day in and day out. Can you say you're working equally as hard for a business you have evenly split three ways?"

My chin drops to my chest, and I link my fingers in my lap. "No."

"Do you think that's fair?"

One shoulder lifts, but I keep my gaze down. "I don't know. It's always been this way. And they've never complained about it, so I've never thought to change it."

"For a minute, I want you to think about how much easier things could be if you had a bigger hand in the day-to-day running of the business and were there. Both your sisters have gotten married and taken honeymoons. Liv has had a baby and Alina may too. Not to mention, Liv's accident."

My spine straightens at the mention of the accident. It's something that I try my hardest to forget. She's had no lasting signs of her injuries, and had I not seen the damage firsthand, I would never have known it had happened. Jameson hasn't been able to put it out of his mind quite so easily, but I'm not entirely sure he tries.

But I do as she says and imagine how much pressure would be off my sisters if I was also able to run the front. Not only would it allow them shorter hours, less stress, and not having to worry about what staff can fill in.

"It would be helpful to them."

"I'm not asking you to jump right in. I'm asking you to start spending more time there, build your comfort level. And you can start that in the back. Is that something you think you're capable of doing?" I know she's only asking to check in. It's not really something I can say no to.

"Yes."

"Good. You should start right away."

My heart gallops as I nod.

"Lean on those who are there and closest to you. Let your sisters support you, and Zach too. Everybody is there to help you, Mazie. Let them."

She knows it's always been hard for me to accept support. Ever since Mom and Dad died, I've felt the need to do it all myself as well as for everybody else. Letting go of control isn't something I do so easily.

"What if I can't stay the whole day?"

"I'm not asking you to get it right away. Or even to stay from open to close. Just what you would consider a routine shift for one of your employees. And again, all I'm asking is for you to *try*."

Chewing the inside of my lip, I nod as I glance out the window. The sun is bright today, and it was fairly warm before I left the house. Tourist season is ramping up as the weather turns nicer. Zach said the small beach at the lake is already packed, and I know the café has been much busier. There's some silly start of summer festival coming in two weeks. We're always jam-packed for that. And now, I'm going to have to be at the café instead of the safety of my home.

Inwardly, I groan. I can't let Dr. Raylinsky hear me because she'll want to talk about it more and, honestly, I want to put it out of my mind until I need to actually think about it.

I know my sisters will be all too happy to have me in their presence, and Zach will gladly bring me by in the morning, if not also pick me up when I'm ready to leave.

No, it's not them that's the issue. It's entirely *me*.

Chapter 20
Zach

I t's been a slow day today. Not that it usually isn't, but things have started to pick up since tourists have started to trickle back into town.

I take another bite of the mouthwatering turkey panini Alina made me this morning. Part of the deal Mazie and I made for her to go to the café was for me to tag along as her chaperone, and Alina's been making my lunch for me as a thank you, as well as Liv making my usual cappuccino. While I've told them it's not necessary, I do appreciate having a meal that's more than just a protein bar and a piece of fruit. And the coffee is always welcome.

Now seems like as good a time as any to have lunch. I've been sitting at this speed trap on the cusp of town for over an hour and have seen two cars.

As my phone vibrates in my pocket, I shove what I can of the sandwich in my mouth and hold it while I dig my cell out.

My brow crinkles as I see Mazie's beautiful face light up the screen. Though I've told her a million times she can call me, even just to chat, she's made herself very clear that she doesn't want to bother me while I'm working.

"Hey, baby. What's up?"

All I hear for a moment are heavy breaths, and I'm immediately on high alert, straightening in my seat.

"Mazie. Talk to me."

"Home...broken..." She says the words through puffs of breath, and I can hear the hysteria in her voice.

"Are you hurt?"

"No."

"I'll be right there." I chuck the rest of my sandwich out the window and flip on the lights and siren, peeling out of the worn-down spot in the grass and kicking up gravel as I go.

Though I've been on the opposite side of town, I make it to Mazie's in about five minutes. It helps that the limits to Juniper Grove aren't that far apart.

I throw open my door and hop on the radio. "Dispatch, I'm responding to a possible 10-62 on Clover."

"We didn't get a call for that, Officer Benning."

"Yeah, it was a personal call." I'm not really supposed to do what I'm doing. All calls and responses are supposed to go through dispatch. But I wasn't about to tell Mazie to call 911 when I've sworn to protect her.

When I get to the front door, it's locked, so I have to dig my keys out. It's one extra step I don't want to have to take right now, but I understand why it's locked. At this point, I'm pretty sure it's just part of Mazie's routine to lock it behind her.

The second I walk in, my heart drops to my feet as I take her in, curled up in a ball in the middle of the living room, rocking back and forth.

Ignoring her normal shoe protocol, I walk right to her and squat down, pulling her against me.

"Shh. You're okay. It's okay. I'm here." I rub my fingertips along her scalp and kiss the top of her head.

She doesn't respond, but she turns and nuzzles her face into my chest. I wish I wasn't wearing my uniform. There are pockets and gadgets and all sorts of things that aren't soft or comfortable.

Taking her shoulders, I push her back and try to look at her, but her head is against her knees again.

It's this very moment that I realize how strong Mazie is as I try to pry her arms away from her legs. They barely even loosen, and while I could certainly overpower her, I don't want to hurt her. Instead, I sigh, drop my hands between my knees, and my chin to my chest.

"I'm going to look around." I run my palm down her curls and stand, walking through the house to find what upset her.

I don't have to go far before I find the culprit. The slider off her kitchen is completely smashed, shattered all over the floor. The glass crunches beneath my shoes as I walk closer, taking a look at the door frame. Whatever happened, the glass was smashed from the outside.

Leaving the room, I take a walk through the rest of the house, checking rooms, under beds, and behind shower curtains. But there isn't a soul in the house besides me and Mazie. It makes me doubt that this was a break-and-enter at all because nothing else is disturbed. At the very least, something else would be amiss, overturned, or a mess. Not just the shattered glass and my girlfriend crumpled on the floor.

I head back into the kitchen to do a little more surveillance, taking a quick peek at Mazie.

It had to have been something hard for the glass to shatter like this. With a furrowed brow, I look around the area, crunching on glass as I try to walk carefully through the area.

That's when I spot it. The white curve of a baseball. Bending to pick it up, I lift it and examine it like it's a foreign substance and not the sort of thing I played with for hours and several years in little league.

And then I lift my gaze to look out into Mazie's yard and my eyes land on the house behind hers. One corner of my mouth tips down as it comes into focus.

Before I can even handle that, I need to get Mazie put back together.

Not wanting to track shards of glass into the living room, I take my shoes off and leave them between the two rooms, hoping none made it this far from the crash.

I squat in front of Mazie again, holding the ball up in my fingers. "I found the offender. It's not quite as scary as you might think."

Slowly, she lifts her head from her legs, still hiding most of her face behind her arms, which are now crossed on top of her knees. Her brows crinkle and lines crease her forehead.

"While I haven't confirmed anything, I'm pretty sure that asshole kid who lives behind you hit this ball straight through your door. Probably the force of the impact and how close it was caused it to shatter instead of just crack or punch a hole right through it."

"He's not an asshole." Her voice comes out tiny and meek.

I raise one eyebrow. "Excuse me?"

"He's only fifteen. And not all that different from how you and Eli were when you were that age."

"Except I'm pretty sure we never broke a window and didn't take accountability."

"Would you have?" It's a good question. And I'm not sure I have an answer. If Jenna knew, she certainly would have made us not only apologize, but likely have found a way to at least financially contribute to replacing it. Had it been *my* mother to find out, I'm sure she would have tried to avoid it, as we wouldn't have had the money to replace it.

I drop my head and lower the ball with a sigh before meeting her gaze again. "He's still going to come apologize to you. Can you get up?"

She nods and reaches for my arm, pulling herself out of turtle mode and standing. Once she's up straight, she falters a little, and I grab her around the waist to keep her upright.

"You okay?"

"Just a little tight and shaky from the anxiety. I'll be fine."

"Why don't you sit, and I'll go get the twerp." With my hand on her lower back, I guide her toward the couch.

I grab my shoes from by the kitchen and walk over to the front door, inspecting the bottoms for any shards before slipping them back on. The screen's open, and I'm halfway out, when Mazie's voice reaches me.

"Zach?"

I turn to look at her.

"Be nice."

A quick roll of my eyes and shake of my head, and I'm heading out the front door. The house is just around the block. Part of me considers taking the squad car, lights flashing and all, but it seems a bit extreme even to me.

I waste no time hopping up the three steps to the door and giving a loud knock.

Thankfully, the little punk opens the door. His face drains and his eyes widen when he sees me standing on his doorstep.

"Does this belong to you?" I hold out the ball.

He swallows roughly and gives a slight nod.

"Did you know that it went right through Ms. Baker's door?"

His head drops and he nods.

This isn't quite bringing me the satisfaction that I was hoping it would. The joy of seeing this boy uncomfortable and wriggling. Instead, he's clearly remorseful.

"This is what's going to happen now. You're going to come over to Ms. Baker's house with me, and you're going to clean up the mess you made. Understand?"

One more nod, and he puts his shoes on and closes the front door behind him. I hand him the baseball, which he tosses onto the grass.

"What's your name, kid?" While the town is tiny, I'm not as up as I should be on all the kid's names. I know this boy's parents are Shawn and Patty, but I couldn't even begin to guess his name.

"Nathan," he mumbles while looking at his feet. He raises his gaze to look at me, fear behind his eyes. "Am I in trouble? Did she call the police on me?"

I hook my thumbs into my duty belt. "Yes and no. You're not in trouble, more than having to apologize and help clean up. And she didn't exactly call the police so much as a friend who happens to be a police officer."

"Is she mad? Miss Mazie is super nice, and I don't want her to be mad at me. It was a mistake, and I was scared I'd get in trouble, so I didn't say anything."

"No, she's not mad. You scared her more than anything. She thought somebody broke into her house." I glance over in time to catch his head drooping further and his shoulders slumping. Without knowing much about him, I can tell he's a good kid who made a mistake and didn't know what to do.

When we get back to Mazie's, he trails behind me like a dog who's just been yelled at for crapping on the carpet. She looks much more put together and is sitting right where I left her on the couch.

"I think this young man has something to say to you." I step aside so that Nathan can't hide behind me anymore.

"I'm sorry, Miss Mazie. I didn't mean to scare you. I knew it broke the window. I heard the glass, and I didn't want to get in trouble, so I ran back into my house and just pretended it didn't happen."

A small smile pulls up the corners of her mouth, and she softens in forgiveness. She knows there was no malintent. "It's okay, Nathan. Thank you for apologizing."

"Nathan's going to clean up his mess now. Right, buddy?"

He's already nodding eagerly.

"What? Zach, no. He's just a child. He shouldn't be cleaning up broken glass." She stands and walks toward us.

I put my hand out low to stop her. "I'll be right there watching him. He'll be okay. He has to learn at some point."

"Shouldn't that be a decision his *parents* get to make?"

"It's okay, Miss Mazie. Dad had me clean up a glass I dropped last week. I'll be careful."

My eyebrows rise on my face as I turn back to her. "See? He'll be careful."

With a huff, she crosses her arms against her chest. "I still don't like it."

I give her a shrug and walk over to the kitchen closet where she keeps her cleaning items, pulling out the broom, dustpan, and vacuum.

She starts to follow me into the kitchen, and I turn around to stop her, pointing at her feet. "Put shoes on."

As though I just gave directions to a child and not an adult, she rolls her eyes and opens the entryway closet, pulling out her house slippers. "Happy?"

"That I'm not going to have to take you to the hospital because you stepped on a shard of glass? Yeah, I am."

Nathan takes the broom and dustpan and starts sweeping, getting the big pieces pulled in first.

Mazie comes to stand next to me, arms crossed like mine. With a sigh, her head leans against my shoulder.

I keep a careful eye on Nathan as he sweeps up the shards, dumps them into the trash, and comes back for more. He's thoughtful with the process, going slowly and getting under both the table and the hutch I found the ball under.

Once he's done, I exchange the broom for the vacuum. He looks around for a moment for an outlet before plugging it in. Either he's been in this kitchen a few times, or his house is a similar model.

Though the vacuum mostly just drones, it does clank through a few pieces of glass.

And just to be sure we've gotten as much as possible, I dampen a napkin and hand it to him. I should give the kid credit, he doesn't ask what to do next, just jumps right in to do it.

He tosses the paper towel into the trash and wipes his hands together.

"Thank you, Nathan. That was very helpful of you." Mazie has to put a positive spin on it. Let's ignore the fact that she was a mess when I showed up, having me ready to beat the hell out of whoever was causing her fear.

"I'm sorry again, Miss Mazie. I promise to be more careful next time."

"Maybe keep your batting to the ballpark?" It's not a suggestion I want to give. Eli and I played baseball in the yard all the time. But I can't have him scaring Mazie again.

He bites his lower lip and nods. "Can I go home through the backyard?"

"Of course, Nathan. Tell your mom and dad I said hello."

His face pales as he realizes he's going to have to tell his parents what happened. When he turns around, he looks the door frame up and down before walking right through the opening, carefully avoiding any of the glass still attached, and runs through the yard.

I turn to look at Mazie and hold her upper arms. "Are you sure you're okay?"

She nods resolutely but doesn't give me a verbal answer.

"You know you can't sleep here tonight. Right?"

Her whole body slumps. It's not that she hates being at my apartment, but she certainly doesn't like it as much as her own home. Who can blame her? She's made this a comfortable place to live, and I often prefer to be at her house. It could be that it's distinctly Mazie and every square inch smells like her and reminds me of her warmth, whereas my apartment has much more of a bachelor pad feel.

She turns to me with wide eyes. "You don't have to work tonight. Right?" There's true terror in her voice, the way it shakes. Though she's stayed with me plenty over the years, she's never been there on her own, and I'm pretty sure if I did have to work tonight, she'd end up at one of her sister's places. Possibly out at Eli's.

"I'm off at five."

"Oh, thank God. What should I do until then?"

"You're welcome to head over there and hang out until I'm done. But otherwise, my best suggestion would be to head back to Three Sticks with the girls."

"This is exhausting. How long will I be put out for?"

I move my hands up to her shoulders and lean back to take a good look at the door. "I'm off tomorrow. Assuming the store has a door in stock, Eli and I can probably replace it then." One thing I'll always be thankful to Paul for. He didn't just teach Eli how to be handy around the house. He took me under his wing and taught us together. While I'm no handyman, I can do my fair share of fixing and replacing.

Lowering my palm to her back, I guide her toward her room so she can throw some clothes in a bag.

"You wore shoes in my house." She glances down at my feet and then back up.

"I'm hoping you'll forgive me this once. In fact, if it will help, after I drop you off at Three Sticks, I'm going to come back to hang a tarp so nothing wild makes its way in, and I'll also mop the floor for you."

She pushes up on her toes and presses her lips to my cheek. "I appreciate that, but I'll do it when everything is back to normal. I imagine you and Eli will be wearing your shoes while replacing the door anyway. No use mopping twice."

There's also something she's not adding, which is that she needs to know that it's done thoroughly and her way. It might bother me if it wasn't just how Mazie is.

I lean against the doorframe as she gathers some clothes. There's a tightness about her body and in her movements. Before she leaves the room, I grab her upper arm and pull her against me, swaying slightly. "Are you okay?"

She drops her bag with a loud thud and wraps her arms around my waist, squeezing tightly. "Yeah."

The single word doesn't bring a lot of confidence, but I know she's processing everything that happened.

I help her into the passenger side of the squad car, closing the door gently once she pulls her feet in and give a quick radio to dispatch to let them know it's all clear. There's a sadness about her and I can't figure out how to get her to open up.

The five-minute drive to Three Sticks is spent in silence. I keep glancing in her direction, but her gaze is trained out the window. When we pull up in front of the café, I throw the car in park and sigh heavily, turning to look at her. "M. What's wrong?"

"I just...I feel stupid and silly."

"What? Why?"

"Because I beyond freaked out and called you in a panic that somebody had broken into the house, all because I saw the door shattered. Never did I even consider that it could have been something innocent. I mean, I know my backyard backs up to a teenage boy's. Why didn't I consider that possibility? I literally saw the door and crumpled to the floor."

I loop a curl behind her ear. "It's understandable after what you've been through. You know that."

"My therapist has been trying for years to get me to have better coping abilities." She looks down at her lap, where she weaves her fingers together. "I don't know. I just feel weak. Like a failure."

Reaching over, I take her chin in my fingers and turn her to face me. "You are neither of those things." It's like a needle pricking through my heart to hear her say such things about herself. Doesn't she see how strong she is, just by all she's gone through in her life?

Mazie clearly doesn't see the important role she's played in people's lives. The way that she's touched and brightened each and every one of our lives.

"Hey." Though I still hold her chin, her gaze has drifted down, but now rises to meet mine. "You know I love you. Right?"

"Yeah, of course, I do, but—"

"No. M, I don't mean in like a *'hey, you're my best friend and I love you'* sort of way. I mean that I'm irrevocably and completely head over heels in love with you."

Her sapphire eyes dart between mine. "How could I know that? You've never told me."

I lift one shoulder. "I don't know. Part of me felt like I didn't need to tell you. That there's no way you couldn't know."

She's silent for a moment, and I wait on bated breath to see if she's going to say the four most amazing words I've ever heard. "I love you too."

Leaning forward, I pull her toward me and press my lips to hers. There's so much more I want from this moment but considering I'm in my squad car and technically still on duty, it will have to wait for tonight.

"Do you want a Coppuccino?"

"No. I'm alright. I'll be back around five-fifteen to pick you up."

She nods silently and climbs out of the car. I watch her walk up the steps to the front door of the café, where she pauses before opening the door and lifting one hand in my direction.

This isn't her favorite place to be, but she'll be safe here.

Now to just swing by my apartment and grab a tarp.

Chapter 21
Mazie

It's been a few years since I've spent the night at Zach's apartment. Or really, much time at all. We used to split movie night between us, but then I bought the house, and he just started coming to me.

Despite the fact that it's been a while, not much has changed. It doesn't really surprise me, as Zach's always been more of a minimalist. Still, it's a tad shocking that everything is *exactly* as I last saw it. Not even the couch has moved an inch.

"Make yourself at home." The word sends a pang through my chest. My home.

Thankfully, Zach called the local Lowes tonight and they have a door in stock. And Steve has a truck that he's letting Zach borrow for the day to transport it from the store, which is halfway to Pineville City, back to my house. Plus any tools they'll need.

Zach takes my bag from my shoulder while I remain stuck in place by the entrance. It's not that his apartment isn't nice. And there isn't really a "bad part" of Juniper Grove, since it's too small for that. But it's not home.

This was not something I was expecting after my appointment with Dr. Raylinsky. I wonder if she'd let me skip a few days at the café while I acclimate to Zach's apartment.

Probably not.

Hopefully, I'll be back home soon.

But then her words ring through my ears. That he's giving up his comfort for my own. My shoulders droop, and I let out a heavy sigh.

I can do this. I can be positive and make the most of this experience with Zach. *For* Zach. He's been staying at my house for a few months now. The least I can do is spend one night at his after he rescued me today and plans to spend his day tomorrow replacing the door.

Out of sheer habit, I take off my shoes. Though, it is a trait Zach picked up from years spent at my house growing up. It's something I took from Mom.

I startle at Zach's hand on my back.

"You look a little lost in thought. It won't offend me if you'd rather be at one of your siblings' homes. I know you've spent more time at their places." His brows pull together, and it makes my heart ache at the fact that he's so giving and understanding of my needs.

I rest my hand on his chest. "No, I'm fine. Really. I was just thinking about my mom."

A look of recognition washes over his face.

With slight pressure against my lower back, Zach leads me over to the couch, sitting and pulling me down so my legs drape across his lap. Immediately, his fingers slide under my pant leg and start swirling against my calf.

"What do you think she'd have to say about us?" His lips curl up on one side and a twinkle skitters through his green irises.

While I'm sure he has a good idea of what she'd say, I can't help but smile as I think about it. "You know she's always adored you. Looked at you like the second son she always wanted but never had."

He opens his mouth to retort, but I hold up a hand.

"I know she loved all of us. That she never complained about having three girls. But I also know at one point, she had hoped to give Eli a brother. You were the next best thing. And in some ways better, because she could send you home at the end of a rough day." I stick my tongue out and push against his shoulder.

But a somberness takes over and the giddiness fades from my chest. "I think...I think she saw something in you, in us, that we obviously didn't. She'd always make small remarks, like how nice you were, how handsome, how much of a gentleman. I think it was her way of trying to plant the seeds in my mind that she saw you were a good person then. And knowing Mom, she had a feeling you were going to turn into an amazing man."

His chin drops to his chest, and he squeezes my leg. I know he misses my parents almost as much as I do. In so many ways they *were* his parents, and he grieved the loss alongside us.

I reach out and press my palm to his cheek, turning his face to look at me. "She was right about that."

The suddenness of his mouth on mine causes my breath to halt for a moment. But I quickly regain my ability to function and loop my arms around his neck, pulling him closer.

Never in my life have I been so consumed by another person. When Zach told me he loved me today, there wasn't even a moment of hesitation or doubt about saying it back. Sure, it's been easy for those feelings to blossom because of the friendship we've had for so long, but part of me thinks I've always been in love with Zach and have just now begun to let myself feel that.

I pull back from him, putting my hands on his chest. "I love you."

His eyes sparkle, and his smile is contagious. I can feel as his heart picks up pace beneath my palm, making my stomach flutter. "I love you too."

Twisting my fingers into his dirty blond strands, I pull his mouth back to mine and start to lean backward, but he loops his arm around my waist and lifts me into his lap.

Before I even have a chance to lower my ass to his knees, he slides his hands under my thighs and stands. I circle my legs around his waist and hold on tight.

He keeps his lips pressed against mine as he walks us toward his room, occasionally extending a hand to keep us from bumping into the wall.

Once we make it into the bedroom, he puts his knees on the bed and lays me backward slowly until my back hits the mattress. Breaking the kiss, he places my hands above my head.

His pelvis presses against mine as he messes around at the head of the bed with something.

There's the clanging of metal on metal that catches my attention. And then a hard coldness surrounds my left wrist. I turn my head to see what it is when the same feeling encircles my right wrist.

I give a solid tug, but there's zero give and the metal digs into my skin. A flutter runs through my chest.

One of his palms slides up my body, lifting my shirt as it skims along my stomach.

"Remember a few years ago, you asked me why I keep this rickety old bed? This moment right here, Mazie. I've dreamed of it for years and pushed it aside. But now, I can live out my wildest fantasies with you."

His eyes darken as he looks me over and his erection presses against my thigh.

The handcuffs clank as I squish down beneath him and clench my thighs together with need. Never would I have thought Zach to be into kinky...anything. Or so domineering in the bedroom.

And even less likely would I have thought that I'd be into it.

But I am. I find myself craving sex and intimacy with Zach more than I ever have with another boyfriend, and not just because I love Zach in a way I've never loved before. It's in the way we come together, the forcefulness of his movements. Like he's just so wild for me that he can't help but be rough and aggressive.

His parted mouth trails across my exposed midriff before he dips his tongue under the waistband of my jeans. A shudder runs through me as his fingers work the button and zipper. As he pulls them down, I shimmy and kick my legs to help him get them off faster.

He raises his head and meets my eye, a smirk pulling at his lips. "Greedy, greedy."

"I can't help it." And it's truly such a weird feeling. I've always maintained control and my faculties in the bedroom. But with Zach, I just let it all go and live in the moment.

It makes sense. He's always been the one to break down my barriers, and now he's breaking down this last one.

"God, it's so sexy the way you give yourself over to me."

Before I can answer, his fingers dive inside me, and whatever words I was going to say come out a strangled moan as I grip the handcuffs and arch my back.

His other hand pushes my shirt up so it's around my neck and pulls down the cup of my bra, sucking my nipple into his mouth.

Zach has always been a giving person. But my God, does he give and give and give in the bedroom. And so rarely does he take.

Like right now, my hand is dying to be wrapped around his hard cock, to be able to feel the affect I have on him. But instead, he has me restrained so I can't touch him at all.

It's almost cruel to take away my new favorite plaything. But this is the side of Zach that has me thinking filthy thoughts throughout the day.

Keeping his fingers inside me, he releases my breast and slides up my body, resting his lips against my ear. "You're going to be a good girl and come all over me. Right, baby?" With his words, he moves his hand faster and hooks his fingers inside me.

My back arches, and a sharp pain strikes my palms as my nails dig in. But all I can do is nod.

Zach has always known me better than anybody, so it makes perfect sense that he knows how to make my body bend to his every will.

He sucks my earlobe between his teeth and puts his free hand up to hold mine. We link fingers for all of a second before he's trailing them down my arm, across my chest, and down my stomach, before closing over my breast.

The moment he takes my nipple between his fingertips is the moment I fall apart. My legs tremble, and I buck against his hand, chasing the feeling. And then I come hard, soaking his hand and his forearm.

A darkness overtakes his eyes as he looks at me. It's feral, and completely intoxicating.

I'm left panting as he pulls his hand from between my legs, examining his arm before licking a trail of wetness from his wrist.

"Mmm. Absolutely delicious." It's only until he's shifted off the bed that I realize he's still completely dressed.

With a feeling of vulnerability, I pull up my knees and close them, my toes skimming the comforter.

Watching Zach undress, my bottom lip lands firmly between my teeth. The way his muscles ripple as he pulls his shirt over his head makes my mouth water.

Though I can see the bulge in his pants, it's much more pronounced once he kicks off his jeans. I've never been more thankful for the invention of boxer briefs in my life. Just as quickly as I appreciate their existence, they're removed from his body.

He stands before me with his hands on his hips like a proud warrior. And he should be. I know he works hard to maintain his physique. To be in what he likes to call "prime bad guy fighting shape." While it feels a bit silly for Juniper Grove, I'm certainly enjoying the fruits of his labor.

As he climbs back onto the bed, his palms trail up my legs, settling on my knees and pressing them apart. He moves between them, lowering himself over me.

The anticipation is so strong, it's like he's moving in slow motion.

After what feels like an eternity, he slips the tip of his cock through my soaking entrance, easing himself into me in one fluid movement. Once he's all the way inside me, he rests his forehead against mine and exhales heavily.

"You feel so fucking amazing, Mazie." He breathes heavily against my neck before pulling out to the tip and ramming back inside.

A jolt runs through me, and my whole body shifts with the force of the thrust. "So do you." Though my sexual history may not be that extensive, I've never been with somebody who filled me so completely, to the point that at times there's a slight burning sensation.

He dips his hips and glides inside me. There're a few more slow movements before a lopsided smirk takes over his face.

Resting on one forearm, he brings the other hand up to brush some curls from my face, and drags his thumb along my bottom lip, pulling it down before closing his mouth over mine.

"If you need me to stop, or if anything hurts, just tell me to stop. Okay?"

With a sharp swallow, I nod. Nothing we've done so far has pushed my boundaries, but he likes to give this reminder every time. It's his way of letting me know that, even though I'm handcuffed to the bed, I'm still in control. While I'm not sure if he does it to be respectful, or because he knows my need to have control over even tiny aspects of my life, I appreciate it all the same.

Slowly, he pulls out until just the very tip of his cock is inside me. Eyes on mine, his hands smooth down my body and wrap around my hips as he slams back into me.

My body jerks with the force and metal clanks against metal.

He continues the process over and over. Some of the thrusts are so hard they're almost painful, but for some reason, I don't want them to stop.

And they don't. Zach doesn't hesitate or slow or ease up at all as he pounds into me. Until my head hits the bars.

So focused on the sheer pleasure I was being given, I hadn't realized how much I'd shifted up the bed.

Hooking his arm around my waist, he pulls me lower on the bed, careful not to overextend my arms. "Going to have to figure out how to get you to stay in place. Maybe ropes would be better next time." He cocks an eyebrow in question, or perhaps to gauge my interest. All of this is so far beyond anything I've ever experienced before; I wouldn't even know where to start. But I trust Zach. With my life.

He reaches next to my arm and grabs a pillow, lifting my hips and shoving it underneath me.

Despite the strange angle that crushes my stomach a little, I'm trembling with anticipation.

Moving closer on his knees, he takes my legs, one in each hand, and trails his fingers up the sides as he drapes them over his shoulders. With a quick kiss against my ankle, he grips my waist and plunges back into me.

The new angle has me writhing and whimpering as his hands hold my thighs and he slams into me over and over.

His grunts, my whines, and the sound of skin smacking skin are the only sounds as he hugs my legs to his chest.

"Holy shit, M." His words are stilted along with his breaths, but I can't even inhale fully.

Every thrust rubs his rock-hard cock along the tight little bundle of nerves deep inside me. He's the only one who's ever been able to make me feel so incredible.

My legs tremble, and I buck against him, chasing after him as he pulls out before gliding back in. There're pinches of pain in my palms as my hands tighten into fists once again.

I pull my bottom lip between my teeth and my eyes slam shut as euphoria begins to crest within me.

But I'm jarred back to reality as Zach drops my legs and leans over me, grabbing onto the bed frame with one hand and using it to move himself harder and faster.

My head tips back with a moan. "Oh, God."

His teeth graze my neck, and he rests his lips against my ear, still thrusting powerfully. "Not quite."

A shiver runs up my spine with his words, and I crumble beneath him. My extremities all tremble, the handcuffs clanking against the iron bars of the bedframe.

The deep groan from Zach has my eyes flying open, just in time to see his head tip back and his face scrunch as he pulsates inside me. He grips my hands in his as he stills, dipping to brush his lips against mine.

"I told you staying at my place wouldn't be so bad." With a grin, he reaches across me for a small towel.

I hadn't even noticed it was there, so caught up in him.

With a gentle hand, he cleans me up, kissing along my stomach as I lie exhausted and stuck in place.

Flopping down next to me, he rests his cheek on his knuckles.

I turn my head toward him with raised eyebrows. "Um." Instead of explaining what I need, I clank the handcuffs.

A devilish smirk crosses his face, and he runs his fingertips from my collarbone straight down my chest. "Just enjoying the view for a little longer."

While I want to give in to his every want and desire, my hands are starting to tingle. Thankfully, I don't have to say anything as he seems to get the message, hopping off the bed and digging through his top drawer. He returns holding a small key and turns it side to side before straddling me and sliding the key into the hole.

With a click, my left hand is set free, quickly followed by my right. I run my fingers over my wrists, which are a bit tender from the strain against them.

Rolling to his side, Zach takes my hands in his and kisses along the light ring the handcuffs left behind. "Hopefully, these faint lines will be gone by tomorrow instead of worse. It'd be a bad day to have to explain these."

"What's tomorrow?" My mind is still in post-euphoric haze.

"Your slider. With Eli?"

I shrink down as my face heats. "Oh, God. That'd be horribly uncomfortable."

"Exactly."

"Well, hopefully I can—" I'm interrupted by a big yawn.

Zach laughs and kisses the tip of my nose before hopping out of bed and hitting the light switch, immediately pulling back the covers and shifting me so I'm underneath them and my back is curled against his chest.

My heart thumps erratically against my breastbone. "What about the doors?"

"All locked. You're welcome to get up and double check if you need to." To enforce his point, he removes his arm from around my waist and shifts away from me.

But a heaviness weighs down my eyelids and my limbs. "No. No, I trust you." A yawn rips through me again, and I shake my head at the end, barely able to keep my eyes open. "I don't know why I'm so tired."

"It's almost like somebody planned on wiping you out so you'd be so exhausted you'd be able to fall asleep easily."

I roll in his hold and press my palm against his cheek. "Thank you."

He leans forward slightly and presses his lips against mine while running a hand over my curls. "You're welcome. Now, go to sleep."

Despite his assurance that the door is locked, and how utterly exhausted I am, sleep doesn't come easily. Looking up at Zach, his eyes are closed, and his breathing is steady. I don't want to shift and wake him, so I chew the inside of my lip and try to fall asleep.

"You're okay, baby. I'm right here. I've got you." His arm tightens around my middle as he pulls me impossibly close.

The steady rhythm of his heart, the warmth of his body, and the protective hold he has on me all help me fall into oblivion.

Chapter 22
Zach

The pounding on a door has me bolting upright. I look around quickly before it registers that it's coming from the front door.

"What's going on?" Grogginess is thick in Mazie's words.

"I don't know. Stay here." Climbing out of bed, I grab a pair of shorts from the floor and pull them on, running a hand through my hair as I pad out to the living room. The bangs start again. "Alright, alright. I'm coming."

I swing the door open and squint as the sun assaults my eyes. It takes a second for them to adjust before I take in Eli's big dumb smile.

"Eli? The fuck are you doing here so early?"

He pushes past me and waltzes right in. "We're replacing a door today. No?"

"Uh, yeah. Later. It's the ass crack of dawn. What are you doing up?"

One shoulder lifts, and he looks around the apartment with his hands on his hips. "Dunno. I was awake. Figured I'd get the day started."

My eyebrows pull together. "You okay, man? That's...not like you."

He walks past me into the kitchen and smacks my arm. "Yeah, totally fine. Had somebody in my bed who had to go, and then I was just...awake."

"Zach? Who's he—" Mazie stops short as she reaches the end of the hallway and sees her brother standing in my kitchen.

My hand covers my eyes as she pulls on the hem of my shirt. Thankfully, it's so big on her it could be a dress.

"Oh. Eli. Um. Hi." Her stilted words show her embarrassment more than her red face.

His eyebrows raise to his hairline as he gives Mazie a once-over and looks incredibly uncomfortable. "Mazie. What are you wear—You know what, never mind. I don't want to know." He holds his hands up in front of him before resting them against the edge of the counter and leaning forward. "Man, this is weird. Not what I was expecting for the morning."

"Does it...does it bother you?"

My hand drops as I scowl at Mazie. Who cares what Eli thinks? He gave his blessing, so now it's too late.

"Bother me? Not exactly. It's just a little weird. Don't worry, I'll get over it. Just need some time to adjust is all. Besides, it's my own fault for not assuming you'd be here. I mean, where else would you have slept last night?" I can practically hear the rest of his thought. *Besides naked in bed with my best friend.*

To end the discomfort this is causing, I clap my hands together. "Okay. Eli, you're way earlier than I thought you'd be. Steve said I could grab the truck around nine. So why don't we go out for breakfast? Mami's?" It's the best local eatery for breakfast. Small-town charm, cheap prices, and the greasy food you want to start your day.

Mazie's eyes light up. I know how much she loves their waffles. "That'd be great."

"Okay. Mazie, how about you go get changed. I'll entertain Eli for a few minutes."

"I'm a big boy. I don't need to be supervised."

"Would you rather I go get dressed in my room with your sister while you stand out here alone?" I cock an eyebrow and tip my head to the side to give him a minute to think about it. For a really smart guy, sometimes he's an idiot.

"Oh. Yeah, no, you're good out here. But be quick, Mae. I'm starving."

"Are you ever not?" She smirks and skips back down the hall. The door shuts with a click.

I turn back to Eli and give him a solid once-over. Though he looks tired, nothing else seems to be off. His behavior lately is what has me concerned. "You sure you're okay with this?"

"Mazie getting dressed first? Yeah."

"Dumbass, you know what I mean. Me and Mazie."

He hangs his head and shakes it from side to side. "I have no issues with you dating my sister. The other things? Hard to swallow, but it's the same with all my sisters. The only difference here is you're my best friend."

"Will you be able to get over it?"

"There's nothing to *get over*." He uses finger quotes as he says it. "It's just an adjustment I haven't made yet. If you're happy, I'm happy. Actually, no. Fuck your happiness. If *she's* happy, I'm happy." He points down the hallway toward my room.

"Ouch. My happiness doesn't matter to you?" Of course I'm just giving him shit. I completely understand where he's coming from.

"Dick."

"Glad to hear you two are playing nice." Her melodic voice echoes down the hallway before she enters. And, of course, she's so stunning my breath halts. Even with her hair thrown up in a ponytail, her auburn curls cascade down and the teal shirt she's wearing makes the blue in her eyes pop.

"Don't we always?" Eli shoots Mazie a wink as she rolls her eyes.

I walk past her, planting a kiss against her temple, and head to change. Quickly. While Eli says he's fine with this, I don't need him getting into Mazie's head again and having her pull away.

It couldn't have been more than five minutes by the time I'm back in the living room and Mazie slides into my side the second I'm next to her.

"You guys ready?"

"Always ready for food." Eli pats his nonexistent stomach.

Grabbing my keys, I hold them up, and Eli nods. A silent acceptance that I'm driving. As we pile into the car, Eli dives into the back seat, which means as soon as we're all settled, I link my fingers through Mazie's.

The drive over to Mami's is short but silent. There's an intensity in the air, and I can't quite tell who it's coming from. For all I know, it's me.

"Morning, all. Have a seat anywhere. Penny will be right over." Susan's pleasant demeanor is welcomed any given morning, but it feels extra nice today.

We find a booth, and Eli and I each sit on one side, leaving Mazie standing at the edge of the table, looking back and forth between us like she's unsure which side to take.

Eli rolls his eyes before putting his hands on the table. "If you don't sit with him, I'm going to."

Her shoulders relax as she slides into the booth next to me, tucking an imaginary hair behind her ear as her face turns pink.

Sometimes the nice thing about a small town is that when you frequent an establishment, they know you. Which I appreciate this morning as Penny walks over carrying three coffees.

"Sorry it's not as good as Three Sticks, but it's what we got." She sets the mugs down in front of each of us, a nervous smile on her face.

I've heard this exact statement any time I've been here with any Baker.

And Mazie being Mazie, she responds exactly as I'd expect her to. "Oh, nonsense. It's just as good."

Penny noticeably relaxes, and her smile widens. She's a good kid who was dealt a rough hand. She was primed and ready for college when her dad got sick. He was the breadwinner for the family, and while her mom picked up a job, it wasn't enough to cover the medical bills and keep the house. So she stayed home and took the first job she could that paid decently and was within walking distance.

She pulls her pad and pen out, ready to take our order, though I'm sure she doesn't need the paper. "Mazie? Waffle?"

"Yes, please. What kind of fruit do you have today?"

"The usual strawberries or blueberries, but we also have some fresh peaches too. There's no sauce or anything with them, but they're pretty tasty."

"Hmm. I think I'll stick with the strawberries. Thanks, though."

I smile to myself, knowing that was going to happen. She always sticks with her favorite.

"Zach? Eggs and pancakes?"

"Absolutely. Thank you."

The only somewhat wild card here is Eli, and only because it depends on how hungry he is at this given moment. When Penny looks his way, he rubs his hands together.

"French toast, scrambled eggs, bacon, and home fries, please." He counts each thing off on his fingers.

Penny nods as she jots it all down and grabs the menus that we didn't even lift from the table as she heads toward the kitchen.

I loop an arm over the back of the booth behind Mazie and start twirling a curl between my fingers.

Though the tension is still palpable, breakfast goes smoothly, with flowing conversation, and Mazie seems at ease the whole time.

But it's not until we drop her off at Three Sticks and grab Steve's truck that I feel like I can really talk to Eli.

I'm about to say something when he cuts me off.

"If you don't marry my sister, I'll kill you with my bare hands. And yes, I realize I just threatened a cop, which is probably some level of illegal." He turns to look at me, stone faced.

"We've only been dating for a few months."

"What is with all you people and your timelines and age gaps and blah blah blah. Excuses. Problems. Might I even say fear. You love her, yes?"

"Yes."

"And she loves you?"

"Also, yes."

"Then what the fuck is the hesitation for?" He smacks his hands on his knees and lets out a frustrated huff.

"It's not typically socially acceptable to marry somebody you've only been dating for a few months." Though honestly, I don't know why. He's right. If you love somebody, then so be it.

"Don't give me that bullshit. You know I don't buy into that. You know my parents. And look how in love they were. Would still be if things hadn't happened. And I know that for a fact." His hand finds his mouth as he looks out the window, and I give him a beat to mourn.

"Besides, you and Mazie have known each other for basically your whole lives. You just added a component to your relationship. I'm assuming."

My eyebrows bunch together, and I glance over at him. Is he asking if we're sleeping together? Or is he asking if we'd already been doing that over the years. Never mind, doesn't matter. He doesn't need to know, nor do I think he wants to.

"And you really think, that if I proposed to Mazie tomorrow, that she'd say yes? You don't think she'd feel it was too sudden?"

He tips his face toward the sky as he considers for a moment. "Mazie's hard to pinpoint in a lot of ways. Never really know how she's going to react to...well...anything. You two could date for three years and she could still feel it was too sudden. That's just how she is. But, yeah, I think she'd say yes."

The silence of the rest of the drive allows my mind to wander. But it doesn't really have to go far. There's not much to have to think about in terms of proposing to Mazie. It's like some part of me always knew it was an inevitability. I don't have to take the time to wonder about what sort of mother she'd be, because I know what kind of mother figure she was to her sisters, and the way she was raised.

We go through Lowes on autopilot, and while Eli continues talking, I barely register what he's saying. I feel like shit about it, especially because I think he's going through some sort of identity crisis right now, but I can't get out of my head enough to listen.

It's not until we're at Mazie's, pulling out the old door, that my attention comes back. And mostly just because he calls me out again.

"I'm serious, though. Are you going to marry my sister? Because if not, if you don't have any plans to do that, you need to let her go before it gets even more serious." He folds his gloved hands over the top of the frame and leans against it.

"I hadn't put much thought into it. Not because I don't want to marry her, but because it just never seemed like an option *not* to. But...you're *sure* you're okay with it? I don't want any sort of change of heart and then she has to choose."

"Nope. All good here. You're good for her. You understand her in a way many don't. As I've said she can be difficult and —"

"She's *not* difficult."

"Okay, I'm sorry. Complex. Sheesh. She's my fucking sister, and I love her till the day I die, but she's a pain in the ass sometimes. And I'm allowed to say it."

Though I grumble at his exclamation, I don't argue again.

"All I'm trying to say is that you *get* her. On a deep level. Things that drive other people crazy don't seem to bother you. And it's a good fit because you're basically her bodyguard anyway. She probably sleeps better at night knowing you're with her."

I nod in agreement, and we carry the broken door and frame to the curb. It's not until we have the new door on the deck that he talks again.

"Just...just don't try to change her little idiosyncrasies too quickly."

"I wasn't planning to change them at all. If she wants to check that the door is locked three times, she can do that."

His face pales as he looks at me. "She still does that?"

"Um. Yeah. You didn't know?"

"She told me she stopped. Years ago. That she had worked through it with Dr. Raylinsky. Fuck, I can't believe she lied to me. To *me*. Of all people." He looks at the ground and shakes his head, hurt clear on his face and in his words.

"I bet she just didn't want to worry you. You know she hates feeling like a burden."

"I don't understand how her grief is a burden for me. You know I don't think she's ever properly mourned their loss? I don't think she's ever let herself truly feel it, though I know she struggles in various ways daily. She just went right into mom mode and never looked back." He scoffs at the thought.

And I give him a minute to level out, before asking a question that I've been dying to know. "Have you? You basically did the exact same thing as Mazie, jumping right into dad mode. I'm not sure you ever truly mourned either. The only ones who seemed to have mourned are Liv and Alina because you two let them. But did you ever let yourselves?"

His head droops as he shakes it. "Probably not. At least not as much as I should have. But it's been over a decade. Feels a little late. At this point, there's so much change going on without them here, that it almost seems like another lifetime."

We start to move the door into place when he laughs. "You know, Dad would be busting our balls for talking instead of just getting the damn door in."

A smile pulls up the corners of my lips. "He was never one for conversation until after the job was done."

"And then it was usually over a beer."

"Even at fifteen," we both say at the same time.

Despite the underage drinking, Paul was a good man. When Eli brought the drinking to his attention, he said that he'd rather we get a taste for it young than go buck wild when we were older. That a little bit while under his supervision was very different than being out at a raucous party.

It mostly worked too. Very rarely did Eli and I over imbibe, and we knew our limits far better than most of our classmates. Enough that when the girls started wanting to party, we were able to supervise and still have a few drinks. It really wasn't even until college that we both let ourselves lose the control we had.

"Well, beers on me when we're done. I appreciate you helping me out."

"Dude, she's my sister. I should be thanking you."

"Guess this is life now, huh?"

"At least we know she'll always be taken care of." He points a finger at me and lowers his gaze. "But if you fuck up, you are *not* welcome on my couch."

"Got it, no couch. That's okay, I'd rather stay at Mansion Penshir anyway. Probably get a whole room to myself."

I laugh and shift out of the way as he throws one of his gloves at me.

But I know the importance of staying and working it out. Of not going to bed angry. It was a conversation we had with Paul before heading off to college. Some of what he called his final words of wisdom before we went out into the big world. It's part of how he and Jenna stayed married for so long. He said if you truly loved each other, nothing was ever worth staying mad about, because neither of you would do anything truly unforgivable. And if you did, then it wasn't a deep love with mutual respect.

It's why I've always taken relationships seriously. And it's why, when I do propose to Mazie, she's going to know that even though loving her isn't a choice, it's one I plan to make every single day for the rest of my life.

Chapter 23
Mazie

It's been a few weeks since Zach and Eli fixed my slider, and things have fallen back into a nice routine. Every morning, whether he's working or not, Zach drives me over to Three Sticks and drops me off for at least a few hours.

I'm mostly still hanging in the back, but I'm starting to be on the floor with Liv while there's a lull. Even though it's not busy, there's still a steady stream of customers. Just not groups of them.

By the time Zach and I are both home at night, I'm exhausted and sore from being tense all day. Tonight is no different, and I'm sitting between Zach's legs while he digs his thumbs into my shoulders.

"So, my mom's coming into town." The way he says it is so hesitant, and I don't understand why.

"How has she been lately?" She moved out to Colorado with his Aunt Helen about ten years ago.

"She's good. But she'll be here for about a week. I was thinking I could introduce you."

I shift away from him and turn around to face him. "Um, are you forgetting that we've known each other most of our lives? I've met your mother, Zach."

"Yes, but now I want you to meet her as my woman."

"Your woman? Really, Mr. Caveman?" One eyebrow raises at his choice of words.

He chuckles lightly and kisses the tip of my nose. "Girlfriend just sounds so...I don't know. Childish? We're not kids anymore. We're full-fledged adults and girlfriend just seems immature."

"It is what I am, though. Unless you want to come up with another word." There's a slight taunt to my tone. I don't expect more at this point, but it also hasn't come up at all in conversation, which concerns me slightly. Is this just fun for him until it's boring?

"I guess maybe I just look at it more big picture. You're mine, as long as you want to be, that is, and the actual title you hold will change over time. I think it's just easier to call you my woman."

Though I roll my eyes, the thought sends a shot of warmth through my body. He wants me to be his, for as long as I want to be.

In the past, I've always scared guys away with my fears, my reclusiveness, my anxiety. Zach not only sees it all but does what he can to support me. He never scoffs, never tries to stop me, and certainly doesn't put me down.

I turn back around and lean against his chest. "So, what's the living arrangement going to look like? She's more than welcome to stay here, but I'm not sure if she'd be comfortable with that."

"I'll have a chat with her before she comes. You seem awfully okay with this."

"Why wouldn't I be?"

"Well...it's just...it's, uh, been about...um." He's not usually one to get flustered. For a second, I have to really think about the last exchange I had with his mom to make sure it wasn't strained.

But then it hits me like a ton of bricks and knocks the wind from my lungs.

I haven't seen her since my parents were murdered. And he's not sure how it's going to affect me that *his* mother is around, but mine isn't.

With a slight shake of my head, I turn in his hold and straddle his lap. My palm runs down his cheek, and I tilt his face up to meet mine.

"Zach. Thank you for considering my feelings. But I know other people have parents. Even though she's not around, I know she exists, and I'm happy you have her, even if she lives far away. *I* lost *my* parents. And it was horrible and tragic, and I miss them every single day. But I can't let my missing them jade how I feel about you having your mom."

"It's just been about the same timeframe is all."

"Has she not been here since?" It seems unlikely, but entirely possible. I know he's flown out to see her a few times.

"She has, but we tended to keep it quiet. I guess I never really knew how to bring it up."

"Have you been talking to her in secret?"

Shame floods his eyes and his shoulders sag. "Not necessarily in secret, but I tried to make sure we only talked when you weren't around. I wasn't trying to hide it or anything; I was trying not to bring you any hurt or pain."

While I want to be mad, that I feel like I should be angry about him hiding it from me, I understand his concern and that he was trying to protect my heart.

"When is she coming?"

"About three weeks. She wants to go to the midsummer festival." He waves his hand through the air like it's just some nonsense to him.

"That festival in particular?" For a town that throws a lot of random and relatively unnecessary events, the midsummer one seems like the least important or exciting.

"Yeah. Something about a memory from when we were kids and the fireworks. I don't know. Why anybody wants to go to any of those insipid things is beyond me."

"You're just salty because you have to work them." Though the force is relatively small, it's all hands on-deck for the events.

"Entirely possible."

"Will she...will she be expecting someone to go with her? I mean, if you're working, that basically just leaves me. Right?" My bottom lip plants firmly between my teeth.

He swoops a curl behind my shoulder and trails his fingers up the side of my neck. "Nope. I told her I have to work and that you guys tend to keep the café open late for customers to come grab coffee or a snack."

While it's not a lie, and we do stay open, I won't be there. Although, with Dr. Raylinsky's new rules, I might have to be. Despite the fact that I might have to be at Three Sticks, I appreciate his forethought to tell his mom I wouldn't be able to be with her. The crowds are something I just can't handle. And he knows that.

It makes my heart flutter as I settle back and snuggle into his chest. My temple rests against his collarbone, and he presses his lips to the top of my head.

Everything about this feels right in a way I never could have imagined. And who'd have thought that he was there, in front of me, the whole time.

The next thing I know, I'm being lifted into the air. Strong arms are under my knees and behind my shoulders.

"What's going on?" The words all slur together.

"You fell asleep. So I'm carrying you to bed."

"The doors." I wave my hand toward the middle of the house, but it drops into my lap as my eyes shut. The days at the café are still wearing me out.

"I'll double check them. Or I'll carry you to each of them. Your choice."

I loop an arm around his neck and snuggle into his chest. "You can do it."

The softness of the bed below me is a welcome feeling, as is the coolness of the sheets. I move to curl onto my side, but Zach presses my shoulders back to the mattress, his fingers working the button on my jeans.

Once they're off, he pulls me up to sit, and lifts my shirt from over my head, quickly doing away with my bra as well. I'm ready to fall back to the bed and sleep naked, but soft cotton falls over my head and to my shoulders and the scent of Zach's aftershave wafts through my nose.

Gently, he lays me back and rolls me to my side, pulling the covers up to my chin. His palm glides over my hair and down my back as he places a long kiss against my temple.

"I'll be right back. I'm going to go check the doors."

"Okay." I put my hand on his shoulder, and it falls to the side of the bed as he moves away.

Though I have to force myself, I stay awake until he curls around me, and his nose runs along my neck before he kisses behind my ear.

"Goodnight, M. I love you."

"Iloveyoutoo." It all comes out as one jumbled word.

But despite my exhaustion, my eyes fly open, and I sit up straight.

Zach sits up next to me. "What's wrong?"

"I was just...when was the last time we had sex?" My face burns as guilt weighs heavily in my chest. It's my fault. I've been falling asleep so early.

"It's been...a while."

"I'm sorry. I'm so sorry. I didn't realize, and I've just been so tired and—"

He cuts me off with a finger to my lips. "Why are you apologizing?"

"Well, I feel bad. We're in a relationship and you have needs and I'm not meeting them."

With a heavy sigh, he takes my hands in his. "Yes, we're in a relationship. And sure, I have needs. But so do you, even if they're not sexual. I'm a grown-ass man, and if you're too tired, or not into it, or just don't want to, I can wait."

My forehead creases as my brows knit together. "Do you not want to?"

"Oh, that's definitely not the reason. I love fucking you. I'd do it ten times a day, every single day, if I could. But we're adults, Mazie. We have lives and careers and other expectations that are placed on us. Sometimes that means you're tired and fall asleep. I'd never expect you to place my sexual needs ahead of your physical or mental ones. And I'd never do that either." He squeezes my hands, but I don't know what to say, because I still feel like it's something I'm not doing right.

"Listen, I know it can be hard with my schedule at times. While I've been lucky to work mostly day shifts the past few months, the nights I'm away are understandably hard on you. And I miss being next to you those nights and while I sleep during the day. But a relationship and intimacy, it's so much more than just sex. And that's what I'm here for. All of it. So if we go through a dry spell, well, it happens. Just know that I love you, and I want to be with you. No matter what."

"You won't get frustrated with me and find it elsewhere? Or end things because we're not being physical?"

He tucks a hair behind my ear and trails his fingers to my chin, pulling me closer to brush his lips against mine. "No."

"How do you know?"

"Because I want this, Mazie. Every aspect of every day. Good and bad. Besides, our sexual chemistry is off the charts, so I have no worries we'll be back at it in no time."

Just the thought sends a shiver down my spine. But instead of giving in to my baser impulses, a yawn has me turning away and covering my mouth.

Being the good sport he is, Zach laughs and leans me back, wrapping his arm around my middle and pulling my back flush against his chest.

"Just one day at a time, M. We got this." He twirls a curl with his fingers in the way that he knows soothes me.

I take his words to heart. Tomorrow is a new day, after all.

Chapter 24
Zach

The station is abuzz when I get in for my afternoon shift.

"What's going on?" I step next to Steve as he looks at the TV.

"Apparently, there's a gunman on Pineville City campus. Something about taking a professor hostage."

All the blood pools in my feet. Eli works there. And I know he's picked up a summer course. But…it's not likely he's there today. Right?

"Are they calling in reinforcements?" Every so often, if Pineville City has something major going on, they'll call out to us for added support. It's rare, but we always respond if needed.

"Not sure. This is just developing. I don't even know how the news is there so fast, because we just heard about it a few minutes ago."

My eyes train on the set in the common room when I see the building they're standing near. A lump lodges in my throat. It's the mathematics building. Eli's building.

Grabbing the remote from Steve's hand, I turn the volume up. "And from what we've gathered, the young woman has an economics professor in the quad just on the other side of this building."

My feet are moving before I've even had time to think about what I'm doing.

"Zach? Where are you going?"

"It's Eli. He's the econ professor. I have to go. I'm going." I'm out the door and in my squad car, lights flashing before anybody can stop me.

As I speed down the road toward Pineville City, I call Mazie.

"Hey, sweetie. I wasn't planning to hear from you until tonight. It's been a pretty good day at the bake—"

"M. Listen to me."

"Okay." There's a waver in her voice as she realizes this isn't a social call.

"You need to be calm. I need you to be calm. You need to *stay where you are*. Do you understand me?"

"Zach. You're scaring me."

With a heavy sigh, I don't hold back. "There's a gunman on PC campus. I have a feeling they're targeting Eli."

There's a sharp intake of air and a whimper cuts down the line.

"But, Mazie, listen. I'm on my way. I'm going. I'll protect him. I promise you."

"What if...what if it's already too late?"

"From what I was able to gather from the news and rumblings at the station, they seem to be at a standstill. This person...I don't know. They're not a mass shooter, so this isn't a random occurrence. There's a reason they went for Eli. They have an issue with him specifically and probably want something from him. And hopefully, I'm wrong." Though deep in my gut, I know I'm not. Some instinct is telling me that he's in trouble.

"I don't want you there either, Zach. It doesn't seem safe."

"There's no other option, Mazie. You know I'm not going to leave it to somebody else or to chance."

"I know," she whispers.

"Tell your sisters, *stay at the café*. I'm serious. Don't try to be there. I don't want to have to worry about you too. Promise me."

"I promise." Though I can't see her, I know the tears are free flowing. She's scared. For the two most important men in her life.

"I love you."

"I love you too." She hiccups the last word and the hysterics start. All I want to do is wrap my arms around her.

Without a goodbye, I click the line dead. If something happens to me, I want the last words she heard from me to be me telling her that I love her.

By the time I pull up to campus, it's blocked off. I park the squad car amongst the rest and head over to the central command. It's easy to find when you know what you're looking for.

"We know they're in the quad that's in between the wings of the building. But that's the only information we have to go on. Not easy to get to without being seen and we don't want to spook anybody."

My brows bunch together. "So what's your plan?"

"Who are you?"

"From Juniper Grove."

"We didn't call in reinforcements yet. You're free to go. We've got this."

"All due respect, I'm almost positive the man being held at gunpoint is a friend of mine. So I'm not leaving. You're welcome to bring up disciplinary action with my chief." I stand my ground, shoulders back, thumbs through the front harness of my vest.

"You got some balls on you, Juniper Grove. Go stand over there and wait for command."

I salute him and walk off. But I don't do as he says. Instead, I snag my bullet-proof vest and head down the road a bit, slipping under the police tape and dashing toward the first building.

One thing about your best friend working at the college is you get an inside scoop and private tours. Yes, the quad they're in can be hard to get to. But not when you know there's a secret entrance in the northwest corner.

According to Eli, it's mostly used by stoners because it's a bit more private than the other entrances and exits, with a short hallway and overhang that hides it from view. It's also somewhere he says kids go to hook up, though the way he's been acting lately, I wouldn't doubt that he knows that from personal experience.

The door is old school, fireproof metal, and I cringe as it creaks when I open it, hoping the sound didn't echo down the hallway.

As I walk toward the light, I'm able to take in the scene while remaining in the dark.

A slight woman with vibrant red hair is shakily holding a gun and pointing it at Eli as tears run down her face. He's standing across from her, hands up in peace. And clearly scared shitless.

While I want to take a moment to digest this, to realize it's my best friend in trouble, it's better that I don't go there. It's better that I keep my professional face on, and let the adrenaline keep me moving.

As I sidestep through the shadows to get into a good position to move in front of Eli, I can hear the woman talking quietly. Not as much as what I'd expect from a situation like this.

"You ruined my life."

"I'm sorry. I didn't mean to."

"I was happily married. And then *you* came along."

"I...I didn't mean to...I don't know what to say."

"My husband is divorcing me and taking me for *everything* I have. I'll be *ruined*. Because of you," she snarls and spits in his direction.

What little composure she had is deteriorating. I have to move fast.

Quickly moving out of the shadows, I go to stand in front of Eli, my hands raised. I don't want to hurt this woman, and I'm hoping we can solve this without firing any weapons.

"Hi there. I'm Officer Benning. I see we have a little issue going on here."

"What are you doing?" Eli hisses at me.

"Shut the fuck up and stay behind me."

"Mazie—"

"Needs her brother. Now shut up."

The woman's eyes are narrowed as she takes in the brief exchange, but she hasn't lowered her weapon.

"Hi. I'm Zach. What's your name?"

Her head turns to the side as she looks me over skeptically. "Nadine."

"Nadine, care to tell me what's going on here? Maybe I can help."

"That asshole ruined my life. So I came to end his." She juts the gun in our direction.

"I'm sorry to hear that. You know I've known him my whole life? He can be a bit of a doofus. Doesn't always make good decisions." Negotiations aren't something often needed in Juniper Grove, but it's something I aced at the academy.

Though I can't feel it thanks to the adrenaline of the moment, I know my heart's pounding away. My vest only protects so much of me if she presses her finger on the trigger.

Thoughts of Mazie run through my mind. What would she do if I died? But they're quickly chased away with how utterly broken she'd be if it were Eli instead. She's lost enough family to meaningless crime.

My mom will be in town tomorrow anyway. I'd hate for it to be to plan my funeral.

This is what I signed up for. I always knew there was a chance something would come to this, that my life might end on the job.

Angrily, she swipes at the tears that are streaming down her cheeks. She seems stably unstable. She's not quite on level ground or she wouldn't be here, but she's not about to lose composure.

"He has three younger sisters, you know. And a baby niece who adores him." I'm trying to appeal to her empathetic side, the part that showed up and didn't just find him and shoot. The part that will hopefully get us out of this mess unharmed.

But when she straightens her spine and tips her chin up, I know I've read her wrong. "You think I care? There are people in *my* family suffering from this situation. His should suffer too."

She's not waiting because she's not sure she wants to do this. She's torturing him a little, playing with his emotions and letting him realize his life could end, that she's in control and he fucked up.

There is no negotiating with her. She's here for revenge. While it seems extreme, you never know how somebody's going to react when their world falls apart. And so rarely do they turn the hatred inward, even if that's where it belongs.

As my mind races for a way to get at least Eli out of this safely, a barely visible red dot lands on the woman's chest. Clearly a SWAT team was called in. And I'm sure the commander in charge of the situation was none too happy to find me not only gone but standing here in the middle of the situation. It's a slap on the wrist I'll take when this is over.

The dot is not something we'd typically have in the sunlight, and sometimes not even when there's an unstable assailant. But part of me feels like it's meant for me. So that I know they're here for support.

"Nadine, you know I can't let you hurt my buddy here. And I don't want to have to arrest you. Or worse. If you put the gun down and walk away from it, I'll let you get a solid punch in."

"Hey!"

"Shut. Up." I grit the words through my teeth. Does he not understand the severity of the situation we're in? Maybe he thinks she won't really do it, that this is just an overreaction. But he should know that sometimes people don't think through their actions when faced with a life-altering situation.

"A punch? You think a *punch* is enough punishment for him?" Though I still have no idea what actually happened, I can wager a guess. They slept together, which her husband then found out about.

"It beats the alternative. Because if you pull that trigger, and shoot my friend, I have to pull my weapon on you. Even if you refuse to put it down, I'm going to have to unarm you, and you'll go to jail."

Her eyes widen for a moment as she considers the consequences, something she probably didn't do beforehand.

But it disappears as an evil grin pulls up her lips. "It'd be worth it."

That's when I realize that the only way for this to end is for this bitch to go down. Eli can be a jackass; I've seen it with my own eyes. But he's also one of the purest people I know. And while he seems to be going through something lately, that doesn't change the type of person he is.

And nobody deserves to die for something such as this.

Now's the time to take action, but the first step is getting Eli out of here. Crossing my right foot over my left, I tilt my chin to my shoulder. "Left."

While I hope he gets my message, Eli's a smart guy. So when I shift slightly to the right, I'm relieved that he follows step. It's going to be slow going to get him to the same exit I came in through. But it's the closest one, and I hope that the darkness will make it harder for us to be seen. If we make it that far.

To avoid risking saying more, I take another slight step. Eli doesn't miss a beat.

Unfortunately, we don't get far before Nadine realizes. "What are you doing? Where do you think you're going?" She takes three steps closer as she shouts, gun raised.

I take a step back, hoping Eli takes at least two, and hold my hands up. "Nothing's going on here."

"You're moving him closer to the exit! I didn't say he could go anywhere!"

She's losing composure.

"Tell Mazie I love her."

I can feel him stiffen behind me. "Tell her yourself."

But I barely hear him as I take a calculated step forward and slightly to the right.

"Don't. Stop."

"You know I can't do that, Nadine. But you can end this. You can put the gun down and slide it toward me and we can all walk away from this."

She tips her head toward the sky and screams.

I seize my moment and lunge for her.

But she's quicker than I am.

A bang rings through my ears as fire rips through my shoulder and I fall to the ground. There's a muffled shout and another shot.

The pain is so debilitating that I can barely breathe, let alone get up, which is all I want to do to see if Eli's okay.

Though my eyesight is blotchy, he comes into view over me, and I scream in agony as he presses his hands to my shoulder.

He's okay. I did it. He's okay.

Chapter 25
Mazie

M emorial Hospital. The second I burst through the doors, everything in my body turns to ice. This place has never brought
me anything but misfortune. It's where my parents were officially pronounced deceased. It's where my sister was taken after her accident.
Thankfully, she walked away mostly unscathed, save for a few breaks and
bruises.

The only thing that could have given this place some saving grace is if
my precious niece had been born here. Instead, she was born at a smaller
hospital that mostly handles births, heart attacks, and breaks. Not like
the level one trauma center they have here.

But now, the love of my life is here with a gunshot wound. That's all
I know. Not where, not his condition, nothing except that he's here.

After Zach called, I talked to my sisters, and we huddled together by
the phone, waiting on bated breath for a call of any kind.

When my phone finally lit up, my heart raced and sank at the same
time. It was my brother's perfect face on the screen. But I didn't know
until I answered that it was him.

"Mazie. I'm fine. Zach got shot. We're on our way to Memorial." Sirens whirred in the background and a loud hum filled my ears as my phone dropped to the floor.

Never, in the history of owning Three Sticks, have we closed shop in the middle of the day. Not until today.

Liv took full control of the situation, gathering my things, quickly closing everything down, and ushering us out. It's just another way she's grown and matured that I haven't noticed. The ability to be calm in a crisis is important, especially as a mother.

We piled into her SUV, Alina sitting in back with me as Liv called Jameson and told him what was going on.

And now we're here, standing in the midst of the emergency waiting room. Everything feels like it's moving in slow motion.

Just as I'm about to walk up to the desk, there's a clearing as the doors to the emergency room swing open. There stands Eli, noticeably shaken, and wiping something from his hands with a towel.

Blood. He's wiping blood from his hands.

I make a beeline for him, ignoring the nurse yelling at me that I can't go through the doors and letting my sisters run interference.

The second I reach him, I throw my arms around his neck. He's here. He's alive.

Putting my hands on his shoulders, I give him a thorough once-over. He's pale, shaking, and there's gauze wrapped around his right bicep.

My gaze lands on it and my pupils widen.

"Just a graze. Needed a few stitches. But I'm okay."

I stare at him intently, not blinking. The one word I want to say I can't get to leave my lips.

"He's alive. He got shot in the shoulder. They said something about through and through and that that's good. Which is how it grazed me.

But they took him to surgery to make sure there's no fragments and that everything is reconnected and intact or something. I don't know, lots of doctor jargon and I'm not in the best headspace."

At that very moment, Alina and Liv get to us and they both throw their arms around Eli.

Immediately, his demeanor changes. "I'm okay. I'm fine. Just a few stitches and I'll have an awesome scar to tell people about." Gone is the scared brother who could have died today, and back is the protector and father figure who needs to keep the evilness of the world from his youngest sisters.

My lips purse together as he looks at me over their heads and shakes his slightly. As far as he's concerned, it's not worth it to let them see how shaken he is, to let them see how close of a call it clearly was.

"Mr. Baker?" We all whirl around at somebody else's voice. A woman in a white lab coat stands before us with a tablet in her hand.

"Yes?"

"You came in with Officer Benning, correct?" She looks down at her tablet and swipes the screen.

"I did."

"He's almost out of surgery. I've been asked to inform you that he'll be in recovery for a little while before being moved to a room. Floor seven, D wing. You can wait in the waiting room there and they'll let you know when he's ready for visitors."

"Thank you."

With a curt nod, she walks away.

"Wait, you came in the ambulance with him?" I turn back to Eli with a narrowed gaze. "How?"

He raises a shoulder and looks at the ground. "I told them he's my brother."

All I can do is nod in response. In so many ways, he's not wrong. And with everything Zach's said, it's likely to be a reality someday, despite the 'in-law' tag it will come with.

My hands cover my face just before I burst into tears. Three bodies and sets of arms wrap around me.

An alarm starts going off not far from us and there's a commotion of people running.

"Come on. Let's get upstairs before he's out." Eli leads the way to the elevator, reaching forward with his right hand and wincing.

Liv steps forward, linking her fingers with his. "You're staying with me for a few days."

"No, Liv, I can't impose."

"It's not a discussion, it's not a choice. You need to rest, somebody to make sure you're taking the medication I'm sure you've been prescribed, and some baby snuggles to bring your light back." So observant, my sister. Though he tried to hide it and act like the same old Eli, she could see he's different. That he's been affected.

To them, he's always seemed larger than life. Like nothing can touch him. Being the next oldest and in the trenches with him, I knew differently. But they're not kids anymore, and they see the reality that life has to offer.

Looking down at our youngest sister, who sometimes seems the most mature of us all, he nods in agreement. "Okay."

Alina throws her arm over my shoulder and pulls me into her side. Everything feels very backward right now. For years, Eli and I were comforting and caring for them, and now they're turning the tables.

The elevator pings open and we silently step in, Alina hitting the button for level seven. I'm thankful the walls of the elevator aren't mirrors, because I'm sure none of us want to see what we look like right now.

When we come to a halt and the door slides open, we heave a collective sigh and step into the stark hallway. A light buzzes and flickers above my head as we stand in a huddle, unsure of our next move.

While these are the types of situations where I usually take control and flourish, today I'm a fish out of water.

Liv steps forward, looking both ways down the hallway, before darting a few feet to the left. "Come on." She juts her head further down from where she is.

Once we reach her, I spot the sign that helped her figure out where to go. The second I see "Surgical Waiting Room," my heart races.

It's just another reminder of what we're doing here. Zach's in surgery. And I have no idea the sort of condition he's even in. Can you die from a bullet wound to the shoulder? I imagine any sort of injury from being shot can result in death.

Will he have use of his arm? There are so many unknowns rolling through my head.

We find a group of seats together and silently sit. Eli's knee bounces relentlessly. I reach over Liv who sits between us and put my hand on his leg.

He looks up at me, eyes wide and filled with fear.

"You okay?"

"No. Not really. It was...terrifying. If Zach hadn't been there...I don't..." He doesn't need to finish for us all to know what he's thinking.

"It'll take a while to process and work through, but you'll be okay. We all will be." Liv looks between the three of us.

It's not just Eli and I who are upset. The most, of course. But Liv and Alina have known Zach their whole lives. He's been like a second brother to them most of that time. And he's been there for lots of the big moments.

I open my mouth to say something, but a nurse comes through the door. "Anybody here for Officer Benning?"

Eli and I jump to our feet. "We are."

"He's in a room now, he can have one visitor."

"You go." Eli practically pushes me forward.

"Are you sure? You were with him."

He's nodding before I'm finished speaking. "You need to go. Besides, he'd want to see you before he sees my ugly face."

I'm wringing my fingers together before I even reach the nurse, who silently leads me through the double doors and down a maze of hallways.

She extends her hand when we reach a room and nods. With a deep breath, I walk in.

Another nurse is in the room, adjusting some IV tubes. Zach is on the bed, eyes closed. From what I can see, he has a bandage peeking out from under the gown on his right shoulder, and his right arm is in a sling against his body.

I take another step closer, and the nurse looks up at me with a warm smile.

"Is he...is he unconscious?" I'm not sure what's considered normal for a situation such as this.

"No. He's still groggy from the anesthesia, so he may be in and out of it for a little while, but he's awake. Was just talking about his girlfriend in recovery as he came out of it."

Heat burns in my chest and spreads through my body, settling behind my eyes. Aside from the bandage and sling, he looks okay. He seems okay. There aren't tubes all over, and nothing's helping him breathe.

Relief sags my shoulders.

"Can I...can I touch him?"

"Of course, honey. Here, come sit. You can hold his hand. And even though he's resting, feel free to talk to him." She sets up a chair on his left side.

Unable to speak around the lump in my throat, I nod and take a seat in the chair, immediately taking Zach's hand in both of mine.

His eyes pop open, and he looks around for a minute before his gaze settles on me, and a wide smile crawls across his face.

"Hi."

Just the one word has the dam breaking, and my eyes overflow as I sob, clinging to his hand as I rest my head on the edge of the bed.

His hand pulls from mine and tangles into my mess of curls, his fingertips massaging against my scalp. "Shh. It's okay. I'm okay."

But it just makes me cry harder, because it so easily could have been a very different outcome.

"I'm sorry I scared you, M. But you know I had to be there."

I lift my face to his, tears free flowing. "Am I supposed to just be okay with the fact that any given day you might be putting your life on the line?"

"That's been my job for years, Mazie. That's always been a possibility."

"But not something I've ever been faced with. It's different now."

One of his eyebrows arches. "Would you have cared less before we were dating?"

"Of *course* not. But now I know what it's like to love you and to be loved by you. I can't lose that. I can't lose you too." I sniffle and wipe the back of my hand under my nose. I'm sure it's less than attractive, but he's seen me at my worst.

"How's Eli?"

"Pretty shaken up, though he'll barely admit it. I guess he got grazed, needed some stitches. But he's okay."

"Good. That's good. That was the goal, Mazie."

We stare at each other for a long moment. There's an intensity, something passing between us. He knows that I'm scared, that I don't want to sign on to lose one more person important to me. But I also know that he'd do it all again tomorrow.

And it's the first time that I question the longevity of our relationship. Because as much as I love him and want him to be my future, I don't know that I can be part of one where the presence of my partner is in question.

Chapter 26
Zach

Mazie's been different since she calmed down. A little aloof, if I'm being honest with myself. I'm trying not to pay it too much mind, but she moved away from the chair when her siblings were allowed in.

Even now, while they're crowded around the bed, she's standing on the other side of the room.

While I continue to participate in the conversation, I track her as she moves about the room, one arm crossed over her stomach, the other picking at her lip.

Disappointment weighs heavily on my chest. Knowing Mazie as well as I do, I know where her head is at. She's likely fighting with herself about whether or not she can do this.

I have zero doubt that she *wants* to. But with her, it's truly a thought of *if*.

Though the thought makes me a bit salty, I do understand it. It's just a conversation we need to have.

My nurse, Sonya, comes in and announces what I knew was coming. "Sorry to say that visiting hours are over for the day. Now, I'm not supposed to do this, but I have a soft spot for first responders because my brothers are all in various branches. You can choose *one* person to stay overnight."

Eli, Alina, and Liv all move away from the bed and say quiet goodbyes. There's a look of intensity in Eli's, and I nod my acknowledgment. This is going to be something that he's continually trying to thank me for, even though it's not necessary.

They each hug Mazie, Alina putting her hands on her shoulders and making sure their eyes meet. "Call me if anything changes or you need anything. Okay?"

Mazie nods and chews her lip. It's refreshing to see one of the Bakers taking care of Mazie for a change.

Once they're out the door, I expect Mazie to come over and sit again, but she doesn't, pacing by the end of my bed instead. She's still playing with her lip, and I can hear a slow hum, but can't make out any of the words she's saying.

"M. Come sit with me." I extend my left hand toward her, and while she hesitates for a moment, she does plop into the chair.

She's a tight ball of nerves, and my heart sinks for worrying her so much.

My mouth opens to say something, but she interrupts, clearly blurting out what she's been going over in her head.

"You can quit, right? I mean, money might be tight for a little while, but I make a good amount. I think we could get by on one income, at least for a while."

I can practically see the gears running at double speed in her mind.

With a heavy sigh, I take her hand in mine and bring her knuckles to my lips. "I know you're worried about me, M. And I'm sorry that I have a job that makes you wonder if I'll come home to you. This situation certainly didn't help. But I'm not quitting. Not only do I love what I do, but I help people. Yes, Juniper Grove is small, but it doesn't matter."

She moves forward and goes to speak, but I continue.

"I was able to save your brother today. What if I hadn't been there? And I know you're scared to lose me and that I'd be just one more person that you love who dies. But you'd be more upset losing Eli, and I know that. You love your siblings more than you can ever love me, and I'm okay with that. Because I'd do it all again to protect any one of your siblings to keep you whole. Because they're who do that for you, Mazie. Not me." It's a realization I came to long before me and Mazie got together. And that's the way it should be.

Whatever family we may go on to have will be the most important thing to her. But her siblings are who she'll always go to when she needs help or advice. Or when I surely fuck up and she needs a shoulder to cry on. And that's the way it should be. They've been through so much together and I'm happy they have each other.

If today has shown me anything, it's that I may *not* always be around. But at least I know Mazie won't be on her own, because she has her siblings.

"Doesn't it...doesn't it scare you?" There's such deep sadness in her sapphire eyes.

"Dying?"

She nods as a tear slips from her eye.

"On some level, yeah, of course it does. Thinking about everything I'd leave behind, especially you. But I knew what I was getting myself into taking a job in law enforcement, even in a small town. You know as well as I do that it only takes one person, one time. If I can save somebody, especially somebody important to you, by giving my life for them, I'm going to do it without hesitation."

"How can you say that when you're important to me too?"

"Because I know it'd be a sacrifice for something greater. Like today, with your brother. The choice was easy, Mazie."

"It just seems so easy for you to be willing to leave me." Her voice cracks at the end.

I release her hands and cup the back of her neck. "Baby, it's anything but."

"Did you even think about me today? About what I'd do if you didn't come home?"

"You were *all* I thought about today, M. And while I know my loss would hurt, I also know you'd never move on from Eli's. Especially because you've never truly mourned your parents. Losing him would only add to it and that's all I was worried about. Do you remember how distraught you were when Liv had her accident?"

Her face pales, as I'm sure she runs through the same memory I do. She was inconsolable. Nothing any of us said helped. No amount of reassurance was enough. She wanted names and numbers and heads on platters. I had to assure her I'd handled everything appropriately, so she didn't get into any sort of trouble. It wasn't until Jameson came that she calmed herself enough to be presentable. And I'm sure that was only because she had to put on the air of being in control.

"I couldn't bear how you would have felt if something had happened to Eli."

She drops her head into her hands and her body wracks with sobs. All I want to do right now is scoop her up in my arms and hold her, but I have these damn IV wires and a broken collarbone.

There's an unsettled feeling in my stomach and a tightness in my chest. And it has nothing to do with my injury or surgery.

"Mazie. You need to decide if this is something you can do. I thought...I thought when we decided to give this a real shot, you had considered all the possibilities and come to peace with it, but it's seeming like that's not the case."

Her eyes meet mine and they're swimming with tears. "I tried. I thought I understood what it could mean. That things were fine as long as we stayed in Juniper Grove and you never had a desire to join the New York State Troopers. But today..." she trails off as her eyes overflow.

My cheeks fill, and I puff out a breath, running my hand through my hair. "I don't really know what to say or where to go from here. I want to be with you, Mazie. All day, every day. For the rest of my life. But I'm not going to ask you to make yourself comfortable with something just for me."

"I'm so confused." Her head drops to the bed, and it shakes with her sobs.

"Maybe...maybe it's better if you're not here right now."

Her head snaps up and the grief on her face tears me apart. "What?"

"I just think that maybe it'd be better if you went home tonight. Got a good night of sleep. Had a chance to really think things over without me being next to you to sway your decision."

"Are you...are you breaking up with me?"

"Never. I don't think I have it in me to end this, Mazie. And I know it sucks to put that on you, but I just can't do it. So if you can't come to terms with my job and the realities that involves, then *you'll* need to end it with *me*." The words burn as they work through my throat and leave a lasting tingle on my tongue.

She stands and bends over me, pressing her lips to mine. The saltiness of her tears infiltrates my taste buds and sends a shot of misery straight to my heart.

"I love you," she whispers against my lips.

"I love you too."

As she pulls away from me, she looks around the room, unsure of what to do. I'm sure she knows if she leaves, it might not be so simple to come back. But she has a lot of thinking to do, and this isn't the place to do it.

My chest is tight as she walks toward the door. While I know it would never be the last time I saw her, I'm worried it might be the last time I see her as my girlfriend. As mine.

When she reaches the door, she gives one last look before she slips out.

And my heart freefalls from my body. My fingers knot in my hair, and I stare at the ceiling, fighting the sting behind my eyes.

It's then that the nurse comes in, a smile on her face that I try hard to reciprocate.

"Any chance I could get something to help me sleep? Hospitals and all that." While I'm exhausted, I don't want any chances of not being able to sleep tonight.

"Of course. I can give you something mild because your pain meds should make you plenty tired. But I'll check with the doctor about what would be best to help you out." Adjusting my IVs, she inserts a needle into the tube and presses the plunger.

Warmth courses through my veins and heaviness weighs on my eyelids.

She leaves and I lie here begging for sleep to overtake me when she returns. "I'm just going to add the sleep medicine."

I nod because I don't want to open my eyes. I want to stay in the darkness behind my lids so I can forget all of this.

Thankfully, the medicine works quickly, and it doesn't take long before I fall into a painless oblivion.

Chapter 27
Mazie

T he second I get through the front door of my house, I drop to my
knees and scream. Why did this have to happen? Why my life?
Haven't I endured enough? Haven't the Bakers been through enough?

After allowing myself a minute to break down, I wipe my eyes and
my nose and stand, locking the front door and putting everything in its
place.

Though I haven't eaten in hours, I'm not hungry. The only thing I feel
is shattering heartbreak.

Without turning on any lights, I walk through the house and climb
into bed, not even bothering to change into pajamas. Every cell in my
body is exhausted. But I can't sleep.

Instead, I stare at the ceiling, the day playing through my mind. My
heart lurches into my throat and beats erratically, a light sweat breaking
out on my forehead.

I could have lost Zach today. I could have lost my brother today. Hell,
I could have lost them *both* today.

From the moment Zach called, it was all I could think about. How was this day going to end and who was I going to lose in the process. Thankfully, I didn't lose anybody.

Though, I wonder if that's actually true. Have I lost Zach? He's still here physically, but has my hesitance, my uncertainty made him question things?

I can't imagine it wouldn't. Even if he says he won't break up with me, will he be different and distant until I pull the plug?

Even though he told me to come home, I shouldn't have left. What kind of message does that send?

I run a hand through my curls and tug at my roots. Nothing makes sense.

A warm shower sounds nice right about now, and I'm about to get up, when my phone rings. Worry courses through my veins like ice, terrified that it's the hospital calling to let me know something happened with Zach.

But my brother's face lights up the screen.

"Eli?"

"Hey, Mae." His voice is quiet and sullen.

"Everything okay? You at Liv's?"

"Yeah. I'm here. They're taking good care of me. Jordanna helps. It's hard to feel anything but happy around that sweetheart." There's always such a lightness in his voice when he talks about her. In so many ways, I feel like Jordanna saved all of us.

"Anything you want to talk about?" There's a reason he's calling me late at night.

"Can you just...can you tell Zach thank you for me? Again."

"I, uh. I'm not at the hospital. Anymore."

"What? Why the fuck not?" Anger fills the line, and I grit my teeth so I don't get defensive.

"He wanted me to take some time to figure out if I can handle his job. The fear of losing him any given day he's on the job."

"You've known he's a cop for years, Mae. Why the sudden change?" Eli's taken on a tone I've never heard him use with me before. It's the parental one of disapproval that he's used with Alina and Liv in years past.

"He could have *died* today, Eli."

"Yeah, and so could have I. And in all honesty, without him being there, I probably would have." My eyes flutter shut and my hand flies to my chest to contain my pounding heart.

"How do I live with knowing that any given day he might not come home?"

"Are you fucking serious right now?" His voice is so loud I have to pull the phone from my ear.

"Why is that not a valid concern?"

"Okay. I'm going to lay this out for you in very plain black and white. And it's probably going to hurt." He pauses, and I steel my nerves and emotions. I know Eli doesn't hold back, but he's never been cruel.

"You're being an idiot."

My breath catches and my eyes fly open. He's never insulted me before.

"Straight up. You, me, Alina, Liv, of *all* people should know that it doesn't matter what you do for a living or where you live. Anything can happen at any time to pull you away from the people you love."

"I know that. So why would I be with somebody who puts themselves at risk every day?"

"For one, you know it's not *every* day. Could it happen any day? Sure. But it's not every day. Not to mention, if something ever happened to Zach in the line of duty, he'd die being a hero and saving somebody. Like he would have done for me today."

My breath catches as he so blatantly talks about Zach dying.

"But you know what else I know for certain? That even if Mom and Dad knew how their story would end, they still would have done everything exactly the same."

"You can't know that." The words barely bleed through my lips.

"I do, though. And if you took a moment to think about it, you would too. They were *happy*, Mae. Maybe they didn't have every single thing they wanted in life, but they had the four of us and each other and that was enough for them. We were all on solid paths, heading toward bright futures. And while I'm sure they would want more time with us, I know they were proud and wouldn't change a thing."

Tears pour from my eyes and drip down my temples, pattering the pillow beneath my head.

"None of us are guaranteed tomorrow, Mae. And while Zach may have a job that puts him at a higher risk than the rest of us, he's protecting and saving people."

I glance to the corner of my room and chew my lip, realizing that he's right and I need to fix things immediately.

"What do I do now? I'm sure he's mad at me." I turn my head toward his empty side of the bed and my hand down the comforter.

"I doubt he's mad. Probably hurt. Just talk to him. But know what you want first. Don't lead him on more if you really can't handle it. That's not fair to either one of you. So make sure you've decided." There's a gentleness to his tone that I don't deserve. It's the one that he uses when he's giving parental advice. It's rare that he uses it with me, and one of the last times was when we had a heart to heart on Liv's porch after I chased Jameson away and nearly ruined my relationship with my sister.

"How do I decide? How do I know for sure?" That's often the hardest part for me. Being sure of my own thoughts and feelings.

"You have to find a way to be. Or at the very least, you need to make a decision and find a way to live with that. No matter which direction you choose to go."

I pinch the bridge of my nose and swipe the tears from my face. He's right. And it's time I put my big girl panties on and evaluated my life.

"Goodnight, Mae."

"Eli?"

"Yeah?"

"I love you. I'm happy you're okay." I clear my throat before my voice cracks.

"I'm not sure I'm okay quite yet. But I'm alive and that's something. I love you too."

The phone clicks off and worry snakes through my mind. I don't want Eli to suffer with this. I don't want it to be a thing he harps on.

Thankfully, he's with Liv.

Everything he said makes sense. I don't need a lot of time to self-reflect. Because in my heart of hearts, I know exactly how I feel and what I want for my future.

Chapter 28
Zach

Waking up in the morning, I feel groggy, but rested. Guess that's what the aid of pain and sleep meds will do. I smack my lips together, my mouth feeling like the desert.

A cup with a straw is pushed in front of me, and that's what I realize I'm not alone.

The green eyes that greet me look sorrowful and worried.

"Hey, Ma."

She runs a hand down my face and pinches my cheek before pointing a finger at me again. "Don't you ever scare me like that again, young man."

A smile pulls up the corners of my lips. "I'm sorry."

Before my surgery, the hospital asked if there was anybody else I wanted them to call, so of course I said my mom. But I wasn't expecting her to show up this early. She was due to fly in tomorrow for the festival, and I was planning to be home first.

"How'd you even get here?" If I didn't pick her up from the airport, who did?

"I'm fully capable of taking a taxi to see my only child in the hospital." Her eyes land on my shoulder and her mouth presses into a thin line.

"Ma, I'm okay."

"I just need a second okay. When you told me you wanted to be a police officer, I made peace with the fact that this might happen someday. Or worse. But to experience it, well, it's a little different." Though her eyes are dry, I can tell she's been crying.

In one day, one action, I managed to put the two most important women in my life through hell. Hopefully, I'll never have to do it again.

When the nurse brings around breakfast, Mom helps me eat, though I insist it's not necessary. I still have one good hand. It's more motherly than she's been most of my life, and I take a moment to relish it.

Having Mom here is a nice distraction from who's missing. Though I've told her I'm dating somebody, she hasn't asked who or where they are. And I appreciate that because I'm not sure I'd be able to tell her.

At some point in the late morning, the doctor comes in and gives me an exam that has me wincing in pain as he lifts my arm and peels back my bandage to check the wound. A scowl resides on my face once he's done, but it quickly brightens with good news.

"I'm sending you home today. Everything looks good on my end, and most patients heal better at home. Lots of rest, no use of the arm, sponge baths only until your stitches are removed. No lifting. I want to see you back in ten days to remove the stitches."

"What about the sling?"

"That's going to be quite a bit longer, I'm afraid. Minimum of six weeks."

My head drops back against the pillow. I'm going to go crazy not being able to use my arm for six weeks.

"Before you're discharged, a nurse will come in and go over bandage changes with you and anything to watch out for. Hopefully, we won't see you again until it's time to remove the stitches." With a small nod, he leaves.

"Fuck."

"Language."

My head tips up as I look at my mother. "Really? At a time like this?"

She rolls her eyes and waves her hands at me as she turns away and starts cleaning up from breakfast.

What the hell am I going to do with myself for six weeks? Especially when I'm not even sure if I have Mazie anymore.

Steve was nice enough to drive me and Mom home from the hospital yesterday. He was also sent to deliver the news that I'm officially on desk duty until further notice, and only *after* I have my stitches removed.

Part of it is because I'm injured, but I'm sure it's also disciplinary for disobeying a direct order from the chief in charge of the active shooter situation. I'm lucky to be getting out with just desk duty. Though, I say that before knowing how long I'll actually be chained to it.

The only bonus is that I can spend tonight at the festival with Mom. She was going to meet up with some friends who still live in the area, but she doesn't want to pass up the chance to be with me.

Town Square is packed, and vendors line the streets with their goods. While I'm trying to be present and listen to Mom talk, my gaze keeps dashing over to Three Sticks, which is completely alit.

Is Mazie in there? Are we over?

She hasn't reached out since I sent her home, and it burns worse than getting shot.

I'm leaning against the back of a bench, sipping a bottle of water as Mom chats with one of her friends and waits in line to get a funnel cake, when footsteps pounding closer draw my attention.

I turn just in time for Mazie to barrel into me, dropping my water and wincing in pain.

"Oh my God, oh no. I'm so sorry. I wasn't, I wasn't thinking straight." She holds her hands up in peace before linking her fingers on top of her head, eyes wide.

"M? What are you doing here?" I put my hand on her shoulder and look around. It's an especially busy year, and I know her anxiety has to be sky high with the crowd. But is that part of it? Is she going to break up with me in a very public setting to keep it calm?

"I had to see you. I called the hospital yesterday and they said you were getting discharged. When I didn't hear from you, I assumed you were giving me space, and I didn't want to interrupt because I knew your mom would be in today, but I needed to talk to you because—"

"M, I love you, but you're killing me here. The point?"

A wide smile breaks across her face, and she bounces on her toes. "I love you."

Relief makes my shoulders sag, but I'm still not sure where she's going with this, so I try not to be too hopeful. "I love you too."

"I'm so sorry that I hesitated for even a second. There's not a single part of me that doesn't want to be with you, that doesn't want to make this work. I was just so terrified, and honestly, I still am. I don't know that I ever won't be. But it's worth it to get to be with you."

Now I'm smiling too. "Yeah?"

She bites her bottom lip and nods.

I close my hand around the back of her neck and pull her against me, crashing my lips to hers.

Her fingers delicately rest against my chest.

"Well, it's about damn time." We pull apart at the sound of Mom's voice.

"Excuse me? Did you just curse?" My eyes narrow as I look at her, and Mazie curls into my left side, her fingers linking with my right hand against my chest.

"I'm your mother, I can do whatever I want. And yes. Because you two have finally seen what's been written in the stars for ages. At least, I'm assuming that's what that kiss and this canoodling is?"

I look down at Mazie, my eyebrows high in question.

Her beautiful sapphire eyes meet mine, sparkling in the moonlight, as she nods.

Dropping my forehead to hers, I close my eyes, breathing her in. For a few days, I was truly scared I was never going to be with her again.

"Do you want to go home? Or back to the café? I don't want you to be out here if it makes you uncomfortable."

She snuggles closer into my side. "I'm good right here."

I kiss the top of her head and start walking again. The fireworks will be starting soon, and the park is about a mile up the road.

Mom snacks on her funnel cake for a minute or two before extending the plate in our direction.

"No thanks, Ma."

"You need to enjoy the little things in life, son." She takes another big bite, powdered sugar falling all down the front of her shirt.

"I won't be heading to the gym for at least six weeks. I think I'll avoid the fried food for now."

"Six weeks? Is that how long the doctor said it'll be?"

"About two for the stitches, and at *least* six for the collarbone." I groan as irritation plucks at me.

"Oh boy. Going to be a long few weeks. You might have to take up some kind of hobby. I don't think you can sit there with nothing to do for that long and not go crazy."

"There are other things that will be more difficult for me in those few weeks."

When her brows bunch together in confusion, I raise one of mine. Even in the darkness, I can make out the slightest tinge of pink her cheeks.

A chuckle shakes my chest, and I squeeze her into my side, kissing the top of her head. There's a weightlessness in my body. It settled in the second Mazie told me she wanted this.

When we get close to the park, Mom perks up, waving a group of ladies who still live here from when she did. She was closest with Jenna, but they had a small group they used to get together with every now and again. Especially the first day of school.

"I'm going to go watch the fireworks with them." She shoots a wink in our direction and heads toward her group of friends.

Mazie and I find a nice spot a little further away from most of the other people, but where we should still be able to see the fireworks as they shoot them off from the lake.

Sitting is more difficult than I anticipate with one arm. But I'm able to settle, pulling up my left knee and resting my arm over the top of it.

Mazie sits between my legs and leans into my left side, careful not to touch my right arm.

I'm dying to wrap my arms around her and hold her close, but I need my left arm to help keep me balanced. And I won't be doing much of anything with the right for far too long. Either way, she fits against me so perfectly.

I lean forward a touch, about to talk in Mazie's ear, when the first firework explodes above her head.

She jumps slightly, but then her face lights up with a bright smile and her eyes go wide. As nervous as Mazie gets around crowds, she's always loved fireworks. At one point when we were younger, she thought they were magical. And in some ways, they are.

A few minutes pass by with the sky lighting up an array of colors and designs, *oohs* and *aahs* all around us, including a few wows from the amazing woman in my lap.

The past few days catch up to me all at once, making my heart pound and my head to spin. None of it's from my injuries or the adrenaline crash, and it all has everything to do with Mazie coming back.

One corner of my mouth perks up, and I lean forward, resting my lips against her ear. "Marry me."

Her whole body freezes, but she doesn't move.

So I say it again, louder. "Marry me."

She shrinks down slightly before spinning around, resting on her knees and holding my face between her hands. "Are you serious?"

"Extremely. I...I don't have a ring or anything. But yes, I'm serious. Marry me."

Before I've even finished talking, she's nodding, and her eyes fill. She crashes her mouth to mine, a little too overzealously, knocking me backward so my back hits the ground.

I pull away to groan in agony, Mazie still on top of me, but she quickly scurries to sit next to me as I grab at my shoulder.

"Oh my God. I'm so sorry. I wasn't thinking. Oh, no, Zach. What can I do?" Her hands hover over my body as she looks at me frantically.

"It's okay. I'm okay." The words squeak out through gritted teeth as I drop my head to the ground and stare at the sky for a minute. In the flurry, I'd forgotten all about the fireworks. I reach my hand out and grab Mazie around the bicep, pulling her down to my good shoulder.

She's stiff and hesitates, but when I tighten my arm around her, she relaxes into my side. While we can't see the actual fireworks at this angle, we can see the sky changing color and hue.

"Are you sure you're okay?" She rests her hand on my chest as she tips her face up to look at me.

"Yeah. We just have to be a little more careful, is all. Plus, I'm probably due for my pain meds."

"Then why are we still here? Let's go get them." With her hand on the ground, she tries to push herself up, but I keep her tight to my side.

"Not yet."

"But you're hurting."

"I'll be okay. I just want to lie here a little bit longer with you."

She resettles into me, and a hum rattles her body.

The booming around us stops and people start to mill about. But we don't move from our spot, and I let my eyes drift shut, enjoying the weight of Mazie against me and the warm summer breeze blowing through the park.

It's not until I feel a presence looming over us that I pop my eyes open to find Mom standing with her hands on her hips.

"You two planning to spend the night here?"

I roll my eyes and sit up, gritting my teeth through the pain, pulling Mazie up with me. She looks at the ground, unable to meet Mom's gaze.

As much talk as she had about being okay with the visit, she's always been a little awkward with Mom. It only got worse when her parents died. She barely knew how to interact at the funeral, though I guess in that situation, most people wouldn't.

Mazie stands and brushes off her fine ass, something I'm going to miss greatly over the next several weeks.

After some adjustment, I'm able to stand on my own, refusing the help of Mom or Mazie. Once I'm standing, I run my hand through my hair, getting it out of my face, slightly out of breath. Fuck, this is going to suck.

"I don't want to interrupt anything, but I was hoping I could talk to Mazie for a minute. Alone."

I tip my head to the side and look down at both of them. "Ma. Really?"

She holds her hands up in defense. "All good natured, Zach."

Mazie turns to me with a tight smile on her face, resting her hand against my chest. "It's okay. I'll, uh, be right back." She pushes up on her toes and presses a kiss to my cheek before walking away.

Though it's pointed at the back of my mother's head, a scowl is planted firmly on my face.

Thankfully, they turn to face each other, and I can see half of each of their faces. But the darkness is too thick, and even squinting, I can't read their lips well enough to know what they're saying.

Mazie nods frequently, not getting a chance to talk too much. At one point, Mom takes Mazie's hands in hers as Mazie looks down and nods. That look, that stance. It's something about her parents.

My spine straightens when I see Mazie's shoulders shudder, but Mom pulls her into a hug, and I realize they're laughing. It lets me release a heavy breath.

A moment later, they turn and walk back in my direction, Mazie putting her arm around my waist and snuggling into my side.

"What was that all about?" I look between the two of them with narrowed eyes.

"Just a little girl talk." Mom lifts one shoulder like it was nothing.

"You're really not going to tell me?" Glancing down at Mazie, sure she's going to spill the details, I get a head shake and smile instead.

"No. What's going to happen now, Zachary, is that you're going to take me home, get your medication, and then take your darling home." She points between the two of us as she talks. For someone who wasn't around much of my childhood, she certainly speaks with a lot of authority.

"And why am I getting my medicine?" One brow arches as I look at her.

"Because you're going to spend the night at her house. It's good practice for the 'in sickness and health' part of the vows."

I jerk back at her declaration. "How did you..." With a quick look down at Mazie, she shakes her head, mouth in a thin line.

"Oh please. I'm your mother. I know I wasn't around a lot for you, working so much, but I knew you two had more going on than just friendship. My only hope was that you'd eventually figure it out, because I was sure once you did, it'd be forever. The only concern was when you two knuckleheads would see the reality."

"Nice, Ma." I sigh and run a hand down my face. "Okay. Let's get going."

While my shoulder is barking, and I'd really like to take the edge off, I mostly just want to curl up with Mazie and sleep. It's only been two nights without her, but two nights too many. The only unfortunate thing, well, besides that I can't bury myself inside her, is that I can't really wrap around her either.

When we get back to my apartment, I let everybody in and walk to the bathroom to grab my pills. There're a few different kinds, pain and anti-inflammatory and antibiotic. I move through to my room and grab a duffel from the closet, tossing some clothes into it. Nothing is easy with one hand, but I manage to make do.

"Are you sure about him coming home with me? I don't mind staying here so you're not alone." I smile at Mazie's kind gesture. It's one I know Mom will refute, but I appreciate it all the same. Especially because I'm sure Mazie would rather be home.

"Nonsense. This place is much too small for the three of us. Besides, he snores so loud, I could barely sleep last night."

"Really, Ma? Sheesh. Do you even love me?"

With a roll of her eyes, she walks toward me and pinches my cheeks. "Of course I do. But you snore, son. Like a train."

I turn around to find Mazie covering her mouth and giggling. "The two of you. My goodness."

"Oh stop. You know you snore. I've always promised to keep it a secret from your future whoever. I just never expected that to be me." Mazie sticks her tongue out at me.

Dropping my bag to the floor, I walk into the kitchen and grab a glass, filling it with water and taking the pain pills out of my pocket. I'm truly not a fan of them, but right now, they're necessary.

"You sure you're good here alone?"

"Of course I am. I live alone, or have you forgotten?"

"I haven't forgotten anything. But this isn't *your* home. I just want to make sure you're comfortable." She really gives me a hard time for trying to be a good son.

"Everything is perfect. I'm going to watch some of my late-night shows, and then I'm going to go to bed. And hopefully I'll get a restful night of sleep." She winks at me, but I shake my head.

"Can we meet you at Three Sticks tomorrow? For breakfast? On the house." Mazie's trying to impress Mom; she never gives things on the house.

"That would be lovely. Just not too early. I like to sleep in these days."

After a brief back-and-forth about time, I give Mom a peck on the cheek and put my hand on Mazie's lower back, escorting her out.

She insists on carrying my bag when we get to her house, so in turn, I insist on checking the doors.

The second I step into her room, she throws her arms around my waist and squeezes, resting her head against my left shoulder.

"I missed you. I know it was only two days, and you've worked nights and been gone for almost as long, but this was just...different. And not just because I was worried about you having some sort of post-surgical issue." I'm sure her mind ran rampant with fear.

"Well, the good news is, I have a little over a week before I'm even allowed back in the precinct. So, you'll have to deal with me all day and night for that time."

"Looking forward to it."

It takes a few minutes for us to find a comfortable position to lie in. It was no easy feat last night either, but now I want to be holding Mazie at the same time. Once we're finally settled, it doesn't take long for her to drift off to sleep, her chest rising and falling gently with every breath.

Taking a curl in my fingers, I twist it gently.

There may have been a hole punched through my shoulder two days ago, and I may have a broken collarbone. But right here, right now, despite the lingering tinge of pain in my side, everything is right with the world.

Chapter 29
Mazie

I scheduled an emergency meeting with Dr. Raylinsky the day after Zach got shot. While I hate to leave him to go to therapy, it's his mom's last day in town, so it works to give them a little more time alone together.

My knee bounces relentlessly as I wring my hands together. Having to relive that day is not something I'm looking forward to.

"So. Zach was shot. Do you want to talk about the day as a whole, or your feelings about it in the aftermath?"

"I think it's all jumbled together." I shake my head as I look at the floor. "I was so terrified when he called. I mean, it wasn't just him in trouble, it was Eli too. There was a chance I could have lost *both* of them. Though Zach assured me he'd make sure Eli was safe, I knew that wasn't really a guarantee he could make. And he didn't even say anything about himself."

I chew the inside of my cheek as I glance out the window. It's an overcast day, almost matching my mood. Not quite sad, but not quite happy either.

"When Eli called and said Zach was shot...I don't even know how I didn't crumple right then and there. My sisters were a huge help, keeping me going, keeping me sane. It wasn't until I laid eyes on Eli and saw he was safe, albeit quite shaken up, that a layer of anxiety abated."

"And how is Eli?"

My brows raze high on my forehead as I meet her eye. "Honestly, I don't think he's okay. And I don't think he's going to be for a while. He's been staying at Liv's, and while he didn't seem to want to be a burden, he's made no move to go back home. I think...I think he's lonely and this scared him. Made him realize he's human and not invincible and just as susceptible to life's crap as the rest of us."

"Do you think he doesn't already know that?"

"On some level, sure. We all had the same big loss. But lately, he's been...out of sorts. I think he's struggling with the fact that he's in his thirties and still single. I know he expected so much more from his life at this point. At the *very* least, to have been a graduate of MIT. Instead, he's an econ professor at the local university. Sure, it's a good school, but it's not MIT."

My heart sinks as I think about all he's had to give up. I was able to follow my dream, Alina was able to chase hers, and now Liv's getting tiny speckles of her dreams as well, thanks to Jameson and his ability to show her not just New York City, but the world.

"But Eli always talked about being a dad, having a family. In fact, he talked about being just like *our* dad, because he truly was an amazing role model. We used to joke that when we had kids, we'd have a leg up on most others for the teen years, having been through it with Alina and *especially* Liv. She didn't make anything easy on us." I glance at the ceiling as I remember my youngest sister, stomping through the house and slamming doors and trying to be just as grown as Eli and I were.

"We've told him, encouraged him, to go back to MIT. To finish his degree. He says he can't, that he needs to be here to protect us, even though we're basically all married off by now. While I'm sure there's more to it than that, likely the bond that forged between us when our parents died, he's never told me. As much as we know and love him, he's a very private and introspective person. There's a lot he keeps close to the vest."

"That's very perceptive of you. How do you feel about that? That your brother and closest confidante hides things from you?"

My eyes widen for a moment as I never considered this before. "I understand it. Aren't there things we all keep to ourselves? Or at least from certain people? I'm not saying he's never told anybody, but it just hasn't been me. And if he feels the urge to keep things to himself, I'm okay with it, because he does so much for us and has given so much. It's the little bit of self he gets to keep."

She nods quietly but doesn't ask any more probing questions. I know that it's up to me to continue wherever my mind feels like leading.

"I'm sorry, I talked a lot about Eli, but it was mostly about Zach being shot."

"Eli's an important person to you."

"He is. And Zach knows that. He told me that he risked his life to save Eli because he knows I'd be utterly distraught if something happened to Eli. That he'd risk his life for any of my siblings to keep me from having to lose one of them."

"Sounds like he understands your bond. And you."

A smile spans my face. So big, I can feel my eyes crinkle. "He does. In every aspect. Even my annoying idiosyncrasies and quirks. He doesn't try to stop them or change them. If anything, he just tries to take some of the burden off of me, so I feel more comfortable and less stressed."

My gaze drops to my left hand. "He asked me to marry him the other day."

When I look up at her, she's grinning. "Did he now?"

"Not officially." A crease settles in my forehead. "Well, I guess maybe officially, since he asked and all. But he didn't have a ring or anything. It seemed impromptu and just what he was feeling in the moment."

"Are you okay with that?"

"I am. Because Zach doesn't do anything without intention. If he didn't mean it, if he wasn't serious about it, he wouldn't have asked."

Which is part of what helped me realize that Zach really was thinking about me and every aspect of what could happen when he went to campus. It wasn't a rash decision based in a frantic moment; it wasn't something he chose, thinking it was what I wanted. He went into it with the purpose and intention of saving Eli because it's what he knew was the best course of action, even if he could have lost his life in the process.

"I'm assuming you said yes."

I nod excitedly. "It took me a minute or two, and I had to make sure he was serious, but I definitely said yes."

"Any thoughts on when?"

"We haven't even talked about it again. His mom's been visiting."

"How is that for you? Seeing his mom?"

"It's..." I hesitate, not really sure how to voice what I'm feeling. A sting settles behind my eyes as I remember what she said to me the other night. "Zach was over at our house all the time growing up. His mom worked a *lot*. While I didn't necessarily know her as well as Zach knew my parents, she was still somebody I was familiar with.

"After my parents died, she moved out to Colorado with Zach's aunt, her sister. I haven't seen her since then." Letting my gaze trail to the window, my shoulders crumple. "I think Zach kept her hidden, thinking it'd be too hard for me, and probably even Eli, to be around his mom after ours passed. He was very hesitant to even mention that she was coming to town, but he wanted to tell her about us."

I have to look up at the ceiling to try to chase the tears away. "The other night, we had a summer festival, and we all went. It's actually where he proposed, during the fireworks."

"Very romantic."

"I've loved fireworks since I was little. There's just something about them that seems so...magical. Like beautiful lights floating in the air and captivating our attention for just moment before another one steals the show. For me, they always had a way of making things not quite so bad. It's part of why I avoided them after Mom and Dad died. I didn't want to feel better. I didn't want to forget for a few minutes."

I swipe my finger under my eye, clearing away the trail of the tear that escaped. "Anyway, Zach's mom pulled me aside to talk to me. And she said she knew my parents would be proud of the woman I'd become, of the success of Three Sticks, of how my sisters turned out. She also said that she knows she's not my mom and would never try to replace her, but as things progress, that if I wanted her help in any way, to just call and she'd fly out. And I just...I really appreciated that she wants to be there for me but isn't inserting herself where she knows my mom would be." I hiccup on the last word and the tears flow freely.

Dr. Raylinsky extends the box of tissues in my direction. Taking a few, I dab at my eyes, wipe under my nose, and then fan my face.

It takes me a moment, but I finally gather myself.

"Well, it sounds like when you're ready, you'll have a lot of support."

A smile peeks out despite the remaining tears. "We really will."

It's a comforting notion. Despite Mom and Dad not being around, when the time comes, Zach and I will be surrounded by family, friends, and people who love us. And that's all we could ask for.

Chapter 30
Zach

Before Mom left a few days ago, I asked for some advice. It's probably a question I'd ask my dad, if I had one.

I clearly jumped the gun asking Mazie to marry me without a ring, without a grand proposal. It's something I need to correct. But I've never gone jewelry shopping before. I've never even considered buying a diamond ring.

So I asked Mom how'd I know which one to get. And while her eyes widened for a moment, and she blew out a breath, a few cryptic words left her mouth.

"You'll just know, honey."

At first, it took me a minute to comprehend what she was saying, because I was sure there had to be more to it than that. But now, as I stand in front of the glass cases with rows and rows of shiny diamond rings, I know she was full of shit.

It takes a lot to make me nervous. I literally just took a bullet for somebody. Yet, standing here has my heart racing and a light sweat breaking out across my forehead.

I'm not worried about Mazie changing her mind, but I want to get this *right*. She's not a materialistic person, but doesn't every girl dream about their engagement ring and wedding? It's my job to make those dreams a reality, even if I don't know what they are.

Part of me considered calling Eli, but I didn't want him swaying my decision. As much as he knows his sister, sometimes his ideas of what she wants are a bit out of left field. Not to mention, I haven't seen him since the hospital. We've both checked on each other, made sure the other was okay, even though I'm fairly certain neither of us are. But we haven't laid eyes on one another.

Just as my eyes start to spin from the glitz all around me, an older blonde woman walks out of the backroom with a smile plastered to her face. I came all the way out to Pineville City to make sure no rumblings made their way around Juniper Grove.

"Hi there. Anything I can help you with today?"

"I'd like to buy an engagement ring."

Her smile brightens, and she clasps her hands in front of her. "Oh how exciting! What kind are you thinking?"

My eyebrows raise; and I pull my lips between my teeth. Am I supposed to know the different kinds?

She giggles and waves me over to the center case, unlocking the door behind it and pulling something out. In each slot sits a plain band with a different shaped diamond.

"These are the various cuts of diamond." She points to the one on the top left. "Round, heart, cushion, princess, oval, pear, marquise, emerald, and radiant."

I run my hand down my face as I look over the options. It's even more complicated than I could have imagined.

"One thing I suggest is to look at them and see if there are any you think your girlfriend *wouldn't* like. Start with process of elimination."

With a nod and sharp swallow, I narrow my eyes and bend to look a little closer. It's easy to eliminate all but the round and oval. None of the others feel like something Mazie would want to wear. So I point to the two of them wordlessly.

"See? Not quite so hard. Next, we'll pick a setting you like."

She puts the diamonds away and pulls out a few trays that are filled with various styles of rings. Now, I can tell what Mom was saying about how I'd know. There are many that are easy to look over, ones that aren't right. Some are too glitzy, some are too plain.

But then my eyes land on one and my heart jumps. Carefully, I pull it from its spot in the tray and pull it closer to my face so I can examine it closer.

The ring itself is not quite gold, but definitely not a silver color either. It's almost...pink. The center diamond is an oval and the sides of the ring are twisted and encrusted with tiny diamonds. It has a feeling of being old, while still being beautiful and new.

Mazie always loved her mom's ring. But I know she'd never want to wear it. Yet somehow, looking at this ring, I feel like Jenna would love it. That it speaks to her as well.

"You look like you've found the one."

My attention is pulled from the ring and back to the woman in front of me. "How do you know?"

"I've been doing this for twenty years. I know the look in the eye when it's the right one. And you, my friend, have the twinkle."

"Well, you're right. This is the one. What now?"

The smile that spans her face makes me wonder why I asked.

We spend the next hour going over details of the ring, including the various 'Cs' of diamonds for the main stone. Things I never in a million years thought I'd need to know or will ever use again. When all is said and done, I pay a deposit for them to create the ring.

One thing I hadn't anticipated is going home *without* a ring today. Nobody warned me you don't walk out with the ring but simply place an order for them to custom craft it.

It kind of ruins my plans a bit.

My intention was to go home, grab some nice clothes, order Mazie's favorite dinner from Antonio's, set the mood with some candles, and get down on one knee before suggesting a movie night. Of *her* choosing.

While the plan might still remain the same, it's not something that I can do for a few weeks. It's frustrating, but there's nothing I can do about it.

The hard part is that I've been antsy, knowing my plans and intentions. And Mazie can tell.

For now, I've been able to pass it off as pain or just not being completely right since the shooting. Truth is, I'm doing better than I would have thought. I had to go in briefly to see the station therapist, who mentally cleared me for work, though until I'm healed, I'm still on desk duty.

Not being able to work is incredibly boring. The small trip out to Pineville City helped break up the day a little. Technically, I'm not even cleared to drive. But who's going to stop me?

It's going to be an incredibly long several weeks if the most I get out of the house is to walk Mazie to and from Three Sticks. She doesn't want me driving yet. Despite my injured state, she still feels safe with me by her side, which is something I don't take for granted.

There're still a few hours until Mazie's done at Three Sticks when I get back to Juniper Grove, so I swing by my apartment to grab some fresh clothes. Though I've basically spent the majority of our time dating at Mazie's house, she's never officially asked me to move in, and I don't want to be presumptuous. It's not so much that I think she doesn't want to, but that she doesn't know how to ask without thinking she'll sound silly.

While I could head over to Three Sticks anyway, I don't want to hinder the progress she's made. Liv and Alina are both happy to sing her praises at the end of the day and how wonderful she did. I'm worried that if I showed up, she'd just gravitate toward me instead of helping the customers, which is the whole point of the exercise.

With some new clothes tossed into a suitcase, I'm about to leave and spend the afternoon watching TV at Mazie's. Not only is her setup nicer than mine, but she has better snacks.

But before I make it to the door, something has me hesitating and instead I flop to the couch, running my hand through my hair.

I dig my phone out of my pocket, wincing slightly at the angle I take on, and hold the device in front of me like I've never used it before. With a deep breath, I swipe it open and make the call I've been avoiding for days.

He picks up on the third ring. "Hey, man." He sounds tired. Not like his usual self.

"Hey. I'm sorry I haven't reached out until today. I just—"

"No, no. I should have been the one calling you. I was trying to let you rest and honestly wasn't sure you wanted to hear from me."

My eyebrows pinch together. "Why wouldn't I want to hear from you?"

"You got shot because of me."

I glance around the room for a second, not really sure what his thought process is. "So?"

"That's kind of a big deal, Zach." He sounds almost...angry. I'm not sure if it's the situation or if it's because I don't seem to be understanding his concern.

"I'm aware. And let me tell you, it hurts like a bitch. But I made a conscious decision, Eli. And I'd do it again."

"Really?" His voice is low and filled with disbelief.

"In a heartbeat."

Silence fills the line, but I know he's still there.

"You fix things with my sister?"

"How'd you know they were broken?"

"The sisters talk. Get used to it." I roll my eyes. He says it like it's something I don't already know.

"Yeah, at the midsummer shindig whatever. I, uh...I asked her to marry me." I pull my lower lip between my teeth while I await his response.

"Did she say yes?"

"She did. I actually put a deposit on a ring today."

"I would have gone with you." He sounds hurt, and I pinch my eyes shut.

"I know. I just felt like I needed to do it on my own. To not be swayed at all by what you think she'd like. It had to come from me and me alone."

"I get that."

"Are you...okay with us getting married?"

"Not only do you not need my permission, but I'm pretty sure I already gave you my blessing or whatever you want to call it." There's a bit of jovialness back in his tone now, and that has me feeling relieved.

"Just double checking."

"More like quadruple checking, but sure."

A smile pulls up my lips and I'm almost certain Eli has one on his face too.

But it quickly passes as more silence settles between us. Hopefully, things will go back to normal, and we won't always have this heaviness.

"Zach?"

"Yeah, man?"

"Thank you." There's so much sincerity in those two words. On a level I've never experienced from Eli. It's a little disarming.

"You're welcome."

The line clicks dead, and I stare at the phone for a minute. I'm worried about him and if he's going to be okay. He's still staying at Liv's, and I know they're taking the best care of him and that Jordanna is a major mood booster, but this was traumatic. Especially for somebody like Eli who's not trained and prepared to take a bullet like I am.

Thankfully, Mazie said he's already reached out to his old therapist. The one who he saw after Jenna and Paul died. He didn't seem to be in the best place *before* this happened. So I'm sure it's going to take some work for him to get back on level ground.

All I can do is keep checking in with him.

And even more frequently when he goes back to his apartment.

He's going to be my brother soon. I was able to protect his life. Now, I need to protect his mind.

Epilogue
Mazie

P art of me feels guilty about having a big wedding since my sisters both went small. But both they and Zach have all assured me that it's not a problem. Liv and Alina both say they *chose* to go small and they support my decision. Zach just wants to see me happy.

Though, part of the reason we went bigger is so he could invite the Juniper Grove police force and Three Sticks staff.

It's not a huge wedding, and the actual ceremony was at Town Hall. But we wanted to truly celebrate, and part of that is because a year ago we learned just how fragile life can be.

While neither one of us wanted to wait too long, I didn't want to get married in the winter. Some part of me has always dreamed of a late-summer wedding. So that's what we did.

Only my siblings were at Town Hall with us, bearing witness to our union. But now we're at Waterfront, the only restaurant in town that has a space large enough to host a wedding. Not to mention, a dance floor.

Having the year to plan was worth it. While we probably could have thrown everything together quickly, it was nice to be able to take our time and evaluate what we wanted and find the right company.

Plus, it gave us all time to heal. Eli still hasn't been the same, and more distant than he ever has been. Sometimes it feels like he's pulling away. From me, from us, from the family. But he always comes back and lets us know he's here, just still trying to figure out his place.

The shooting affected him more than any of us could have anticipated, and at the suggestion of his therapist, he took a sabbatical year from teaching. The idea was for him to find himself again, to recenter and refocus. But as far as I can tell, he's just spent a lot of time alone. Or possibly with women, I'm not entirely sure.

His therapist suggested some travel too. Possibly going back to visit Cambridge and MIT. But he wasn't willing to leave the area.

He saw his own mortality, realized how much he hasn't experienced yet. And it messed with him. The biggest problem with that is that he won't let any of us help him.

We all try, we hover. But the more we push ourselves on him, the more he pulls away. It's a very fine line and delicate balance.

I watch from the edge of the dance floor, champagne in hand, while Alina waddles over and sits next to him. She's eight months pregnant and has been a great sport so far today. While I told her she could pick a different dress, wear something she'd be comfortable in, she insisted on wearing the Matron of Honor dress that I fell in love with. She and Liv are wearing the same thing, being co-matrons, and they both look beautiful.

My hairs stand on end when I feel a presence next to me.

Zach looks amazing in his tux. He fills it out so perfectly; I can't wait to go home and tear it off him.

"Glad to see Alina's finally sitting down."

A smile pulls up my lips. He's become even more protective of my sisters now that he's "officially their brother," as he likes to say. Though the protectiveness jumped the night he re-proposed.

He doesn't really like that I call it that, wanting it to replace the initial proposal since it was sudden, unplanned, and he had no ring. But it's part of our story, and I love both times equally.

"Hopefully, she'll have some water too." With my lips pressed together, I look around for Cam. Finally, my gaze lands on him as he weaves through the people, a pair of slippers in one hand and a glass of water in the other. I jut my chin in his direction. "Looks like Cam's on top of it."

"He's really turned out to be a good partner for her. I was skeptical, I'll be honest."

I smack the back of my hand against his chest. "You didn't give him enough of a chance."

He narrows his eyes at me. "I seem to remember you doing your fair share of that with your *other* sister."

"And I learned my lesson."

"So when Eli finally finds somebody, you'll welcome her with open arms?"

I wave my hand as I turn back to the dance floor, my attention landing on Liv, Jameson, and Jordanna as they hold hands and sway to the music. "Of course not. No girl will ever be good enough for my brother."

He sighs next to me and laughs lightly, wrapping his arm around my shoulders and pulling me against his side as he kisses the top of my head.

His fingers trail down my bicep and graze my breast, causing me to look up at him with raised eyebrows.

Even a year later, one thing he likes to continually mention is how terrible it was to only have the use of one hand at a time. And right now,

I know he's thinking that during that time, he wouldn't be able to have an arm around me and be holding a drink in the other.

His chest puffs out with a deep breath, and he pushes up to his toes.

My chin drops slightly as I cant my head to the side, mentally preparing for whatever he's about to tell me.

"I threw your birth control away this morning."

With wide eyes, I take a slight step to the side so I'm standing more in front of him than next to him. "I'm sorry, you did what now?"

"Tossed it right in the trash."

"And you didn't think to, I don't know, consult me? See about when I want to start a family?"

His gaze lowers, and his eyes bore into mine. "If I have my way, you'll be pregnant by the end of the honeymoon."

Heat rushes my cheeks and it's suddenly extremely warm in this wonderfully air-conditioned event hall.

Wrapping his arm around my waist, he pulls me into his chest. "Why wait? Why delay starting the family we both know that we want? It took us long enough to realize our feelings for each other, so why put off anything else?"

I rest my cheek against his chest. "You could have talked to me about it first." Truthfully, I'm giving him a hard time, because I'm completely packed for our honeymoon, and didn't put my birth control in my luggage. While I wasn't exactly going to spring it on him like he did me, I was going to mention at the resort that I forgot it at home to see how he felt about it.

But that's a pivotal difference between us. I'm a thinker, and he's a doer. Over the past year and a half of our relationship, we've brought out the other side in one another much more than we ever did while being just friends.

Before, I would have fixated on the birth control, the discussion, the repercussions of stopping it. Now, I had made the decision alone and planned to feel him out before going for it.

With my fingers linked around his waist, I lean back. "You sure you don't want to, I don't know, enjoy married life a little first?"

"Very sure. We're not exactly travelers, M. What are we going to do? Sit around the house and just be husband and wife? No, I'd rather start our family."

Two years ago, the idea would have made me hyperventilate. One year ago, it would have sent me into a downward spiral of fear. But now, I'm all in. To an outside observer, it would all seem so sudden. A few months of dating before getting engaged, a year of engagement before tying the knot, and then getting pregnant as soon as possible.

What they don't know, didn't get to see, is all the years of buildup, of denial, of circling each other. The foundation was poured long before the frame started to go up.

And while I was hesitant at first, I can see that everything is happening exactly the way it's supposed to.

Epilogue
Zach

While still being attentive to Mazie, I've been trying to keep track of Eli all night. This is the first time he's been around a large group of people in a year.

He took the whole school year off, and while I honestly have no idea what he did with himself besides wallow in misery, he was still present. Sure, there were the occasional times that nobody would hear from him for a week or two, when he'd skip family dinner. But he was battling some demons and assured me he was okay.

Seeing him here, I believe him.

Though he's not being the life of the party like he used to be, he's had a smile on his face all night. He's danced with his sisters, with Jordanna, and at one point, I heard him making inappropriate passes at one of the waitresses, who smiled and laughed it off.

To somebody who doesn't know Eli, he'd seem just as he's always been. But I can tell there's something missing. The light is gone, the urgency. The silliness. He's on his way back, but he's not there yet.

It took him a while to be normal with me. But the more I assured him everything was fine, that I'd do it again, the more he started to believe me. Once I was fully healed and back on the streets, he came around more.

It felt like the longest year of my life, both with the healing process, which wasn't over once the sling came off and the wound was healed, and processing the event. Mazie had nightmares at first. Thankfully, she confided in me and in Alina, who had gone through her own bout of nightmares. With the help of Dr. Raylinsky, we were able to overcome them.

Worrying about Eli took up a lot of the time. There were family meetings to talk about how he was doing. Everybody had varying insights, as he seemed to tell different people different things. All in all, the overwhelming theme was that he was going to be okay. Not just because he said it, but because he made progress and just needed time to process the event on his own and with the help of his therapist, who he assured us he was seeing weekly.

The only concern I have for him now is the family aspect. He wants it, and he realized that much more intently after the shooting. Some of the prep for the wedding was hard on him. He's the oldest and has no prospects. Though he tries to hide it from his sisters, to put on the happy face of a brother who's proud of them and loves them, a part of him is jealous.

It was one conversation over the winter when he really laid it out for me. I hadn't realized how intensely he was feeling it, but like a lot of things with Eli, he keeps it close to the vest until he's ready to share.

It's why when he gets up from his chair and heads out to the patio, I want to follow him. But I'm intercepted by a party guest and have to put on my host hat. I glance around quickly for Mazie to see if she can take over, either with Fran the dispatcher or checking on Eli. When I finally find her, I know I won't be interrupting. She's having a sisterly bonding moment, all three with their arms around each other.

"So happy for you and Mazie. She's a sweet girl. The whole Baker family is. Such a shame what happened to their parents. You know I handled that call?"

My attention focuses back on Fran, who's almost a foot shorter than I am, at the mention of the Bakers. "No. I wasn't aware of that."

"Truly horrific thing. They were such lovely people. Very wholesome. And they did a great job with their children."

I lift my gaze back over to Mazie and her sisters, the corners of my lips pulling up. "They certainly did." But my stomach plummets when I realize I was on my way to check on Eli. That he's not back and not part of the Baker hug.

"I'm so sorry, if you'll excuse me. I'm needed for...something." I shift away before she can stop me and head straight for the door to the patio.

As soon as I push through the door and into the thick night air, I know I'm too late. Because all I can see is his back as he follows after a redhead toward the parking lot. While I want to be mad that he's basically skipping out on my wedding, I can't blame him for becoming overwhelmed, even if it does look like he's just chasing tail.

I hope he knows what he's doing.

The End

Elijah's story comes next!

Coming January 2024
The following is an unedited preview and subject to change.

Chapter 1

Elijah

Sitting in my chair, my ankle crossed over my knee while I nurse my beer, I look around the crowded room. All three of my baby sisters, happier than I've ever seen them. And they deserve it, all of them.

But I can't help but wonder when it will be my turn.

I've sacrificed a lot for them, more than they'll ever truly know. I did it all willingly, and I'd do it all again exactly the same way.

The look on Liv's face is worth it all. Her giant toothed grin, that I'm not sure I've every truly seen on her before Jameson entered her life. He's good for her, he gives her things that nobody else would have been able to. Our father raised me to protect my sisters, that it was my job to look out for them. I've always taken that to heart, and probably looked over

Liv a little more than the others. She got the raw end of the deal, having Dad for the least amount of time.

I didn't like Jameson at first, didn't trust him. Nowhere near as much as Mazie, I could see a *little* hope for him. I think Dad would have liked him, would have seen from the beginning what it took me too long to notice. But he grew on me, and now he's probably my favorite of the brother-in-laws. He's able to give Liv the life she always wanted. She'd never leave our small town, the rest of us, but he kept his apartment in the city and takes her regularly. Gives her that small taste of city life that she's always wanted but never would take for herself.

He'd protect her to a fault, lay his life on the line for her if ever needed.

Watching them now, Jameson keeping Liv tucked tight into his side with one arm, holding their two year old daughter, Jordanna, in the other, solidifies every past decision, everything I sacrificed.

"Hey, big bro. Mind if I sit?" Alina plops into the chair next to me, her swollen belly causing her to lean back.

"Of course, LeeLee." The nickname I gave her as a baby has stuck. Much like Liv's. Most of us have nicknames for one another that only we get to use.

"I can't stand much these days. Liv said it gets better but I'm not sure she can be trusted."

"Oh certainly not. We all know that Liv is a known liar."

We both smile and chuckle lightly. If it's one thing Olivia is known for, it's her total honesty. Even brutally. She doesn't hold back, she has no filter.

"You only have a few weeks left. Feeling ready?"

Her eyes grow wide as she rubs her belly. "No. Not at all. But Liv said that instincts just kind of...take over. I know she feels like a screw up sometimes but Liv just...I don't know, has her shit together somehow."

"So do you, Alina. And if there's one thing the Baker clan can do is take care of others, of their own. You'll be great."

"Yeah but a baby? Eli, that's not the same thing as another adult, or teenager."

"You're right it's probably easier than taking care of the three of you was."

She reaches out and smacks my upper arm, causing me to laugh before I start peeling at the label on my beer bottle. "You can do this, Alina. And you have Cam. Not to mention all of us. We're all here for you, just like we were for Liv when she had Jordanna."

"I know. I do. Big changes and all." She runs a hand over her stomach again.

"Hey wait, where is Cam? Shouldn't he be here like rubbing your feet or something?" I straighten as I look around the event hall for him. It pricks at my nerves that he's not doting on my sister.

"He went to get my slippers from the car and try to get me a pitcher of water from the bar." There's a sheepishness about the way she admits it.

Knowing Cam is doing his husbandly duty, I sit back and look over at Alina. She'd be upset if she knew I still didn't completely trust Cameron to not leave again. "Your slippers? Really? You're co-matron of honor. And you're going to wear slippers? With your dress?"

"I'm eight months pregnant. Mazie's lucky I'm even *in* a dress." She runs a palm over her stomach and looks at me incredulously.

"Fair point I suppose." I tip my beer in her direction and take a swig, looking out over the large gathered crowd.

Mazie's the first of the sisters to have a big wedding, the younger two opting for small and intimate, though they certainly could have gone big.

Especially Liv. I'm sure there was no expense that Jameson would have spared to give her the best day ever.

Though, I do understand the reasoning behind Mazie and Zach wanting to truly celebrate with all their friends and family. A near death experience will do that to a person. His mom and aunt even flew out from Colorado. I've been lucky enough to mostly avoid them. I'm not quite the conversationalist I used to be. Not since last summer.

It doesn't help that there's still a level of guilt that I feel for getting Zach shot. I'm sure his mom blames me for that, and I don't think I could stand the look in her eyes. These thoughts have been swirling around more and more as the ever looming start of classes nears.

The year off wasn't quite as rejuvenating as I'd hoped it would be. I wanted to go back with a fresh outlook on life, feeling renewed and safe and really all I did was mope about my apartment. While a lot has changed, I don't feel any different.

Zach thinks I spent the year drinking and sleeping around. He's mostly wrong. Sure, I enjoyed the company of a woman or two, but not nearly like I'd been doing before. Having a gun pointed at your face can make you change that side of you real quick.

"Oof." The complain from Alina draws my attention back to her and I see her pressing a hand against her lower back.

Concern pulls my brows together. "You okay? Do you need me to get somebody?"

I'm halfway out of my chair when she puts her hand on my forearm. "No. I'm fine. This one's a kicker. And his favorite thing to beat on is my kidney. It hurts sometimes."

Flopping back to my chair, I laugh lightly and finish off my beer, looking out to the crowd to find Mazie and Liv. Some habits die hard, and that includes keeping track of my sisters any time we're in public.

It's not just for protection, it also helps me learn about them and notice things that they may not bring up. Like the fact that Liv's pregnant again. She hasn't revealed yet, and I'm sure it's because she didn't want to rain on Mazie's day. But all week she's been clinging to Jay more than usual. And through the past several days she's teared up far more than is normal for Liv. Not to mention that she's a little green around the gills. I've taken care of her enough when she's sick and picked her up drunk from enough parties to know what she looks like when she feels like she's going to puke. And that look keeps creeping to her face.

Two sisters, moms or at least about to be. And I'm sure Mazie's not far behind. I can't help but feel like at some point it all went wrong for me. Part of my job was to are for them and guide them. I can't do that not being a parent. I can't protect them from things I know nothing about.

"You ready for classes to start again?"

My spine straightens as I adjust in my chair. The thought has been circling in my mind for weeks now. "Honestly, I'm not sure."

"I guess that makes sense. Have you been on campus since last year?"

I roll one shoulder and tip my head to the side. Despite the air conditioning, I have to pull out my collar, feeling a bit overheated. "Um, not yet."

"Probably going to be a tough transition. Do you feel ready for it?" She's not trying to make me uncomfortable or upset me in any way. One of the things she's worked on with her therapist is becoming more direct, especially when talking about somebody else's struggles. It's part of how she and Cam keep themselves open with one another.

But it's rubbing me the wrong way. Mostly because I don't want to talk about it. My own therapist would say that I'm deflecting and avoiding, and maybe he's right. But I can't sit here a moment longer.

Thankfully, at that precise moment I spot Cam weaving through the groud, a pair of pink fuzzy slippers in one hand and a pitcher of water in the other.

"Hey, uh, Cam's on his way back. Mind if I leave you in his capable hands?"

"Of course. I'm sorry, did I say something? I didn't mean to—"

"No. No, you're fine. Just a little warm. Want to get some fresh air."

The look on her face tells me she doesn't believe a word of my bullshit but she'll never call me on it. Actually, none of my sisters will, not even Mazie.

I find the closest door that leads to the outdoor patio and make a beeline for it. Fresh air will help.

Acknowledgments

W hat an amazing journey it's been to get here. With that, comes many thanks.

To my amazing husband and children:

Another book, another thank you. I still cannot begin to truly show or explain my gratitude for all that you do and all the ways you continue to support me on this incredible journey.

I truly could not do a single aspect of this without you. Having you by my side every step of the way means so much to me.

I love you!

To my amazing duo; AK, RL:

You are my rock solid team. There for any question, any confusion, any help I need, I know you're there. It's amazing to have found not just great writing partners, but friends.

To my fantastic PA team; Chanel and Kalie:

I know I'm a solid pain and am so far behind on my game it's sad, but you are patient and wise and helping me go the extra mile. I'm so thankful for you both!

To my incredible street team:

Thank you all for you continued support of me and my work. It's amazing to have readers who enjoy my work enough to want to promote it for others to read. I'm truly thankful for you all.

To my amazing editors Mackenzie and Beth:

This book would not be what it is without you and your input. Thank you for helping me learn how to be a better writer, adjusting my words, and most importantly, keeping my voice my own. And especially for your beautiful words as you read through it.

Thank you to the amazing **Fine's Fine Designs** for my stunning cover!

To my ARC team: Your time and effort does not go unnoticed. Thank you for reading my novel before it hit the public and for your gracious reviews. I know it's not always easy to find the words, but it's all so appreciated.

And most importantly, to the readers:

Thank you for taking a chance on me. Whether you're an established reader of mine, or new to my books, I'm so thankful for you. I write because it's my passion, but I publish because I want to share my words with all of you. I hope you enjoyed reading it, as much as I enjoyed writing it.

About the Author

Shayna Astor is a romance author who loves writing sweet love stories, with a lot of spice. When she's not writing, she's probably watching The Office with a cup of coffee, spending time with her kids, or playing video games with her husband.

Stalk me for all the latest updates, teasers for upcoming novels, giveaways, and all the goods on what's coming next!

Instagram @shayna.astor.author

TikTok @shayna.astor.author

Facebook Group Shayna's Coffee Corner

Website www.shaynaastor.com